IT FOUND ME
Sequel to Amazon's bestseller,
THE HOUSE ON POULTNEY ROAD

BY

STEPHANIE BODDY

First published in Great Britain in 2014 by SCAMPS

ISBN 978-0-9928092-7-0
EBOOK 978-0-9928092-8-7

<u>Acknowledgements</u>

My biggest thanks goes out to each and every supporter and avid reader of my debut novel, *The House on Poultney Road* (and other short work in between that one and this). To the 13'372 followers on Facebook (to date) who encourage me to keep writing and to come up with the next story – of which I have about five synopsis ready to get to work on.

I thank my gorgeous husband, Elliott for putting up with being lonely some nights and being plagued with horror movies on others. My Mum and best friend Yvonne, who isn't only my number one fan, but also one of the main characters in this book. A big thanks also to my Mother-in-law, Lorraine who believes in word-of-mouth publicity and really should get a job in PR. To the Silver Fox who has proven that agents can be very nice people indeed and to my cat Gizmo - for just being cute.

I thank all of those family members who have a place in my haunting tale (especially Jake who 'basically is the book'). To all those who are still with us and those members who have already passed over - I'll see you all on the other side and I'll give you a mighty tight 'thank you' hug then.

Love you all.

Steph x

P.N. Some names, places and descriptions have been changed for legal reasons. Although *It Found Me* is based on a true story, the said information will fall between fact and fiction throughout this re-telling.

Fear stems from an origin hidden deep within your mind, where your nightmares and darkest thoughts are locked away. Sometimes, when you're alone at night, they surface or if you're a writer - like me - you write those thoughts down and offer your readers the key. S.Boddy

That tunnel, the one we must always walk through and is one of my deepest fears. Because death itself brings it. Because the night that will cover my eyes won't let me see the way. There's nothing more terrifying than walking in a dark single way without stopping nor turning back. Not knowing our goal, nor smelling or hearing a thing. The limbo void tunnel. Luis Vilela, competition winner.

Prologue.

It was dark inside the house; like a cloud was settling above it, waiting for the storm. Whether it was grief that the family carried or the dark atmosphere growing within its walls, it seemed to be getting worse. It was only when the nights came that it bothered Ellen. During the day she could keep herself busy – both physically and mentally – but at night there was nowhere she could hide. She knew that without Richard she would need to leave the house; that eventually she would have to turn her back on the one place that she and her family had called home for more than seventy years. But selling a house that was ridiculed due to the scandal of her late husband's delving into the paranormal was as difficult as you might imagine. No one wanted to be haunted, regardless of whether or not they believed the supposed stories.

During the time she and her family lived at 106 Poultney Road, playing with Ouija boards and organising séances, Ellen was constantly asked, "Why don't you move?" The answer was simple back then; money. The Camps could not afford to sell up and still live in the area, and with the kids at home they did not want their financial problems to affect their lives. Now that Richard was dead, leaving her enough money to move to a peaceful house in the country, the answer to those questions was not as simple. It was not only that the reputation of the house was difficult to cover-up, but Ellen believed that her husband may have some spiritual connection to it. It was not an easy decision to consider when she thought that her late husband's ghost may be trapped within those four walls; she would be leaving him alone to spend an eternity with the malevolent spirits he had once awakened.

She kept the television on until late. The lounge was so full of memories that she didn't need to be distracted by

3

game show hosts or soap operas. Her thoughts were consumed with her own stories. Of her three boys growing up, arguments they shared over games of charades bought a smile to her face. The television was only ever used as a distraction; a deterrent from the other unexplainable noises she might hear elsewhere in the house.

A photograph of Richard and herself was resting on her chest. They were together on a beach in Devon just a few short years ago. Finally, she put the photograph down, and wiped dry her tear-soaked cheek on the back of her hand. He had only been gone a couple of weeks and although she was coping, the pain was not getting any easier like everyone kept telling her it would. Picking up the remote control, she took one last look at Terry Wogan and turned off the television, leaving the room in darkness. She moved quickly to the light-switch and turned it on. The beam filled the room with amber light that comforted Ellen's dark imagination. Although she tried, it was difficult for her to forget what went on inside the house, the activity that she knew resided there.

She moved quickly through the house, turning all of the lights off and checking that the doors were closed and locked. Not that crime was particularly high, but it made her sleep better. Ellen had not been fortunate enough to make it through a night without waking for one reason or another, either an urgency to go to the toilet which she would almost always try to ignore, or because of the nightmares.

Don't think about it, she reiterated to herself over and over. If she tried not to think about the things that went bump in the night, then she would be less likely to be plagued by nightmares. She called them nightmares, but most of the time she knew all too well that she was not asleep, the most terrifying things always happened after she had woken up. The first nightmare, or day terror as some often refer to them, had been the night following Richard's

4

death. The memory of that night came back to her, unbidden.

It had been about two o'clock in the morning, February 3rd, 1982 when Ellen was torn away from her sleep. She had been dreaming of times passed, when she had first met Richard and they had both been young and beautiful and getting old wasn't something that either one of them needed to consider. They had both been carefree, Ellen more so as Richard always carried the burden of his best friend's death on his shoulders. It hadn't been his fault but he had, for some reason, always blamed himself. He had been there and his conscience always reminded him that if he hadn't of allowed himself to have been distracted by that evil man; he could have, might have – possibly - been able to save his friend.

Something unbeknown to her had torn Ellen from the sunshine and the comfort of her husband's embrace; had shaken the life back into her, and she had woken resentful, angry at whatever had disturbed her beautiful dream. It took her longer than usual to realise she was awake, at home and in bed. It seemed more and more that her dreams, nightmares and day-terrors were all to roll into one big routine and she often needed to knock some sense into herself. Falling back to sleep after such awakenings had always been easier with her husband lying by her side. But with Richard gone and the left hand side of the bed empty, it took her longer to adjust and a while to stop herself from having an anxiety attack. She reached out for the small lamp on her bedside table and flicked the switch. Nothing.

"Damn electrics," she cursed beneath her breath. It happened more often than she would like to admit, although she had never missed a payment and she had gotten Richard to change the bulbs more often than they had needed to be changed. She convinced herself it was some dodgy wiring that needed replacing. Along with cutting back the trees and replacing a broken fence panel in the back garden, it was just something that she needed to add to the odd-jobs list; *or rather the things that now Richard has gone, are left for me to sort out*, she thought, somewhat resentful. If Richard had been there, she would have woken him up and made him fix it then and there to show him just how frustrated she felt. But he wasn't there, and he would never be there to hear her impatience again. But that was not to say that he was not still watching her, still able to hear her irritation and that was what infuriated Ellen the most. All the years they had been visited by spirits, poltergeists or whatever else you may want to refer to them as, now that she hoped and prayed that Richard's ghost may return, she waited in vain.

What was that? In the silence of the room, she heard the floorboard creak. It sounded as though it came from the far end of the bedroom. Her pulse quickened as she opened herself up, making herself more alert. "Who's there?" She asked into the darkness; there was no reply. She sat up in bed, wearing only a pale floral nightdress, her arms pressed against the bitter cold air around her. She shivered, *someone's stepping over your grave,* she recalled Richard once saying. The very thought brought on yet another shudder that moved through her whole body.

It came again, this time the creaking floorboards were accompanied by the gentle bump of the wardrobe door closing softly, "Hello?" she asked again, but she wished she hadn't. Without moving anymore than she had to, comforted by the soft blanket that shielded her lower body, she reached into the small drawer of her oak bedside table where she knew she had a small torch hidden. *It better bloody be there, you better not have put it somewhere for safe keeping, Richard,* she thought to herself. Without too much kafuffle, she felt the small, cylinder handle of the torch. Flicking the switch on the side, she panicked, thinking it would not work, but immediately a small beam cut through the darkness, opening up the room for her to see.

She moved the stream of light frantically around the room, darting from wall to wall. There was nothing but drawers, a small varnished oak dresser to her left and the wardrobe in front of her. Her anxious behaviour almost caused her to miss the darkness that stood beside the tall piece of bedroom furniture – almost. She drew a deep breath as she tried to calm her breathing and her behaviour, which was not proving too rational. She followed the beam along the wooden floorboards and across the pile of clothes she had left on the floor at the end of her bed before she reached the foot of the wardrobe. She drew in a deeper breath, searching for the courage to retrace her motions back to the dark figure that was there just moments before. The light fidgeted beneath her grip like dancing fireworks, her trembling hand moving the light along the border of the wardrobe.

That was when she saw him. It had been months since the last time he visited – if that's what you call a haunting. It seemed that when Richard had grown sick, the entity left the house alone. Ellen thought it was out of respect perhaps or, slightly more frightening, because he knew it would not be long before Richard joined him on the other side. She had tried not to think too much about him returning to her – she knew of all of the entities that he had contacted over the years, it was the man in black she would least like to be locked inside the house with. His spirit had haunted Richard for so many years, she automatically presumed that his torment would die the day that Richard did; but who was it that now, accompanying her in her bedroom, stood at the end of her bed? She considered speaking. *It could be Richard,* she thought for a moment, but she knew that he would not do something that would scare her. She felt the heat at the top of her neck rise into her head and a small droplet of sweat trickled down her neck and to the top of

7

her spine, tickling her and causing her to arch her back away from the sensation. As she did, the torch light moved along the edge of the wardrobe, almost all the way to the top. But along with the chipped and scratched oak panels, Ellen also saw the outline of a long black cloak and a top hat. Her stomach somersaulted, and she had to swallow hard to prevent herself from throwing up. If she ran, he would not need to chase her. He would already be waiting for her downstairs, preventing her escape. If she hid beneath the covers, he could turn and make his way up the side of the bed and suffocate her beneath the sheets, but if she stayed, not taking her eyes from him, she would be in control. She would watch his every movement, predicting any advances. Her eyes began to swell, warm with moisture, and the taste of salt washed itself on her lips. If there was any time she needed Richard, it was now. But he was not there, he was not even watching over her. Her eyes soon blurred from tears, as they began to flow more freely, soaking her skin. She wiped her bare arm across her face, smearing the wetness that was there, but allowing her to see clearer. When she focused again, back on that dark space next to her bedroom wardrobe, it was empty – no shadows, no dark figures, just a vacant space. She could now see the painting her husband once made of a tiger in the depths of a mangrove swamp; a painting that she had always adored. Besides the ferociousness of the animal's teeth and the beauty of his burnt orange fur, its eyes were soothing, like the animal had been tamed. She didn't know why, but at that moment all the fear that had erupted inside her melted away and froze into a sense of grief. She no longer cared who was with her in the room; she didn't care what was haunting her and the house she lived in. She knew that there must be someone somewhere looking out for her.

Grief overcame her, and her mind soon forgot about the dark figure that had visited her that night. Her fear was dissolved by the eyes of the beast that was looking out for her through her husband's painting. Protecting and distracting her from the shadow that had passed across the room, through the wooden door and into the depths of the house.

Chapter One. Impossible.

"You should take the test again," Eric suggested as he made his way to the bedroom door, tugging his jacket from its hanger. "It's just not possible. You probably read it wrong." Eric made about his morning routine as if it was just a normal, bitter February morning. "Anyway," he continued, "the doctor told us both that children wouldn't be on the agenda for us after Jane. You're not pregnant."

Yvonne sat herself on the edge of the bed whilst she listened to her husband convince himself that he was not becoming a father for the second time. A pointless remedy as she knew her body better than anyone and that against all odds, she was pregnant with a second child; thirteen years since her last. She knew the day she married Eric that his priorities revolved around the office, and although sometimes it made life lonely, in all, Yvonne respected him as he strived to keep a roof over his family's head and maintain a comfortable life for them.

Shortly after she had given birth to Jane, Yvonne suffered from gallbladder stones which, in 1975 was considered an extremely serious illness and one that she almost lost her life to. There was no quick fix and given just minutes more, her life would have tragically ended. She had major surgery to have them removed. She was told that she would not be able to carry another baby and that the operation she had made it fairly impossible for her to conceive. They had digested the information well and accepted that their family finished at three. But when, in early February 1983, Yvonne was late for her period and the usual morning sickness crept its way in, she was as shocked as Eric to discover she was pregnant. Though a little less hostile than what he was. This was not to mention that having a child at thirty-eight made Yvonne an older mum; she had a long nine months ahead of her.

Eric walked back into the bedroom once he had combed back his dark hair and kissed his wife on the forehead.

"I'll see you this evening," he said, "and no more baby talk." Eric skipped the stairs, grabbed his keys from the bottom step and made his way out of the front door, closing it behind him.

Yvonne sat for a moment, taking in her husband's reaction. It had not surprised her; Eric was a business-man with only business on his mind. Another baby would be last on the list of things he wanted. She was hardly expecting jumps of joy. Although not planning for another baby, Yvonne had become acquainted with the idea even though she had only hours to get used to it herself.

They had lived in a three-bedroom house, situated south of Hertfordshire in a quaint village called Sawbridgeworth. A peaceful home they had shared with their daughter, Jane and their abundance of pets for the past thirteen years. The early years of marriage had been tough, Eric's business had experienced its fair share of ups and downs and they had been close, more than once, to losing their home. Chasing deals and prospective money was in Eric's blood; he had learnt the trade from years wheeling and dealing on London markets and it was never long after slipping from the road of success did he pull himself back onto it, accelerator pushed down, hard.

The Camp's were financially stable with no reason not to be happy with the prospect of a new baby. Of course, there could be complications, but nothing Yvonne was not prepared for. She decided the best plan of action would be to make an appointment at the doctors that afternoon; to find out if Eric's simple dismissal was the right attitude to have.

*****

12

Yvonne's appointment was at eleven o'clock, so she dropped Jane off at school in the next town and made her way to the shops close to the surgery. She wanted to grab the evening's dinner before taking another test in the presence of a doctor. Although more than a decade had passed since she was last pregnant, Yvonne was in better shape than she had ever been, playing football three times a week, rivaling her husband's sportsmanship. She felt positive about her situation and was prepared for whatever the doctor might say.

"Yes, Mrs Camp, you're pregnant, congratulations." Dr Griffiths was a sternly man, dressed in a marl grey suit and seemed honestly pleased to deliver the news. "This is your second child. Correct?"

Yvonne nodded.

"Some people prefer not to but because of your age, I recommend that I have you booked in for a screening, just to be sure everything is OK with you and the baby. It's best to be on the safe side," he asserted with a grin, ever-so-slightly slimy. Yvonne had not ever been keen on doctors since a vile experience in the sixties, and Dr Griffiths was not helping her mind-set.

Yvonne nodded once again, slightly put off by Griffiths' emphasis of her being an older mum. OK, so she was not similar to the other young Mums boasting nativity and precaution, but she was confident and self-assured. She was actually feeling better than she ever had and decided to agree to the screening, even though she knew all the same that she would keep the baby regardless of its result.

She left the surgery in a daze. The sun was shining and the bitter air made its way through her jacket as she pulled it tightly around her, leaving an ever-so-slight chill beneath it. She was beaming with pride and could not believe she was pregnant, against all odds. She could not wait to tell Jane, she knew how excited she would be to have a little sister, but breaking the news to Eric may not be as easy.

She imagined him sitting as his desk, taking calls and making orders. He often used work to distract himself from reality and from the grief he still felt for the loss of his father. Each time Yvonne brought Richard's name up in conversation, Eric would flinch as though salt was being rubbed into the raw surface of an open wound. Work was a place his mind could escape reality and encourage prospective thoughts on money-making ventures, and making money was something Eric was good at.

She decided to take herself home before making the call, but would stop at the baby boutique en route. There was no harm in looking.

She got home around two o'clock, put away her shopping, made herself a coffee, black, no sugar, picked up the receiver and dialed that ever-familiar number.

"Hi Juliet, it's Yvonne. Is Eric about?"

"He is," the secretary replied, "I'll just try his line." Juliet was the perfect candidate for Eric's assistant. Fresh out of college, she was eager to learn, perceptive and not afraid to make the tea or coffee whenever she was asked, which was often.

"Hello?" Eric's deep voice echoed down the receiver. "Yvonne, you OK?"

"Yes, sorry. Eric I have some news. I'm pregnant." Yvonne blurted out. She knew it was the best way. There was no point beating around the bush with Eric, he would usually lose concentration by the time you hit the second sentence with his mind on work or ears on the radio.

"Oh, for God sake! Not more of this baby-talk? I told you this morning, it's not possible." He said quite matter-of-fact.

"Well it is possible; I've seen Dr Griffiths and it's confirmed. We're having another baby."

There was silence down the phone. Neither of them spoke. Twenty seconds must have passed before Eric broke the silence. "Well, I don't know how you let this happen. I

14

need to go there's a call I have to take," and with that, Eric hung up the phone.

"Unbelievable." Yvonne said whilst shaking her head at her husband's rather bizarre reaction, "But utterly typical." A smile grew across her face as she rubbed the palms of her hands across the flat of her stomach.

*****

Pregnancy the first time round was a doddle. Jane came in at six-pounds, five-ounces, comparable to a bag of sugar but much healthier, and had grown into a real bundle of joy. Sleeping patterns were easy with no early morning tantrums and therefore, Yvonne and Eric had been introduced to parenthood quite smoothly. After the shock of being a Dad some thirteen years since his last child, Eric had grown fond of the idea and Yvonne only grew fonder.

Jane took the news well. She was repulsed that her parents were still 'doing it', but she loved the idea of having a baby brother or sister to look after. No doubt she saw pound signs flash before her eyes at the thought of all the prospective babysitting she could do. Jane was a stunning young woman, and took after the Irish on her father's side. She had long black hair which sat neatly upon her petite rounded shoulders, and a desirable hourglass frame that was already the envy of all her secondary school friends. Her huge, sultry blue eyes and delicate nose, sat within a face which resembled a Disney Princess. Unfortunately, Jane had grown out of the cute little baby image she once had and was quite the madam, but an only child and being spoilt rotten had encouraged her mini attitude. She had a harem of friends at the school for girls she attended and was at the top of every boy's dating list.

Yvonne's parents, Mervyn and Elsie, were thrilled with the news that they were going to be Grandparent's again. Ellen was excited; it was uplifting news to receive after such a devastating loss in the family. Although Yvonne was extremely kind to her mother-in-law, keeping regular checks on both her and Flo, Ellen was happy with an excuse to spend even more time with her family. Yvonne and Eric had three nieces. Nicole and Hannah from Yvonne's brother, Ben and his wife Mary, and Claire who was Robert and Janet's daughter. Everyone was very excited to learn of the new addition; no-one loves anything more than the sweet smell of a new born.

Yvonne had left it three months before sharing the news, what with the heightened risks at the early stages, and so it was almost six months after Richard had died from lung cancer that the family was told the news of Yvonne's miracle baby.

*****

The months soon passed and Yvonne's bump grew and grew. The pregnancy was fine throughout without any hiccups and all the scans came back clear. With pleasant cravings of cherries and melon, Yvonne was pleased she was not sucking on coal or chewing straw.

The Camp's prepared for the new arrival, and during the nine months they moved into number one-hundred and thirty-eight Greenmay Close. Yvonne fell in love with the house as soon as she clamped eyes on it. At the end of a quiet cul-de-sac in Sawbridgeworth, the four-bedroom house had a large front garden and a drive with large patio doors covering the frontage. Inside was a good sized lounge at the back of the house which boasted an open fireplace and patio doors that opened onto the large back garden. Perfect for a dog, Yvonne had thought. They had lost their beloved family dog, Sandy, a few months back and the bareness of an animal-free home meant it would soon be time to adopt another furry companion, but she knew better than to suggest that when Eric had only just accepted the patter of human feet into his life. At the front of the house was a very bright dining room with a large floor to ceiling sliding door and open arch into a beautiful country-styled kitchen. There was also a man cave to the front of the property, or as a woman would refer to them, a garage. Upstairs had four double bedrooms and a huge family bathroom with an American-style Jacuzzi bath and double sink. It was the perfect family home.

*****

Yvonne was in her third trimester when she first experienced the pain. It started in her lower back and would travel across her stomach as though her uterus was being choked.

"Eric, something doesn't feel right," Yvonne said as she sat herself up in bed, bringing her knees up, trying to relieve the discomfort.

"What is it? Is there something wrong with the baby?" Eric asked as he jumped from the mattress to his feet.

"I'm not sure," Yvonne continued before it hit again. This time with vengeance and she screamed out and grabbed her husband's forearm. "Eric I need a doctor."

*****

Dr Griffiths came as fast as he could but by the time he arrived at their home, the pain had passed. Yvonne had moved to the sofa in the lounge downstairs with her feet up on the footstool.

"Could it be contractions? The pain was almost unbearable." Yvonne asked, allowing the doctor to examine her.

"I doubt it. Baby isn't due for seven weeks. I would put it down to Brixton Hicks although they don't usually cause the level of discomfort you're describing. Keep a diary if the pain returns and make an appointment at the surgery, but now that mother and baby appear settled, I'll let you get back to bed. Keep your feet up for the next few days," Dr Griffiths said as he shot a look at Eric, "your turn to look after mum."

Eric walked the doctor to the door, thanked him for his time and closed the door behind him. He was relieved that his wife and baby were fine. He knew how useless he was with emotions and feelings but he knew that he could not live without his wife and he hated seeing her in pain.

When he returned to the lounge, Yvonne had fallen back to sleep; a light sleep no doubt, but he could not leave her downstairs by herself so he checked on Jane, who was out for the count—that girl could sleep through a World War— and made himself comfortable downstairs with his wife, in the armchair opposite her.

*****

"I'm going to have our baby early." Yvonne said as she made about her morning routine. "I just know I'm going to go into labour close to your Dad's birthday."

Eric stood still momentarily, looking at his wife, absorbing what she was telling him.

"I hope not, that would mean you'll be a month early. You're not due until fifteenth of November; whatever makes you think it will happen sooner?"

"Just a hunch," she replied as she popped the toast from the toaster, buttered it and smothered it in rich, crimson strawberry jam before handing it to her husband. "Anyway, nothing for you to worry about. And don't mention anything to Jane as I don't want her getting too excited too soon. It's hard enough composing my own excitement."

No sooner than her name was mentioned, did Jane appear in the kitchen.

18

"Mum, can I have some toast too, but mine with marmite please. I don't know how you eat that stuff Dad, all that sugar in the mornings can't be good for you." Jane said, eyeing her father's breakfast.

"OK, I think that's my cue to leave. See you both tonight. I have football training after work so dinner for seven would be great." Eric grabbed his keys and left for work.

Yvonne dropped Jane at school as usual but decided to follow doctor's orders and take it easy, so she made her way home. Deciding to spend the day with her feet up, she parked and ran in to the local newsagents to get herself a couple of trashy magazines to distract her from the boredom of doing nothing for eight hours. Although she was past thirty weeks, she didn't look or feel frumpy at all. *You're all bump* people kept telling her, but she was the same with Jane and, in fact, left hospital in a size ten dress she had kept back from the sixties. She hoped that with another month or so of expansion left inside her, her body would be as supple as it was thirteen years ago – maybe that dress would be thrown into her overnight bag as it was before. *Fingers crossed* she thought.

Mooching through the reads on offer, Yvonne nosed through all the typical maternity books with obscene titles on the front promoting stories about teenage pregnancies, celebrities and other such trash. Someone lightly tapped on her shoulder, causing her to jump in her skin.

"Sorry to startle you, how have you been?"

It was Rachel Downing, the owner of their house before they bought it.

"Hello, sorry I'm a bit of a nervous wreck, these days," Yvonne said as she gestured towards her protruding belly, "it's the hormones. How have you been keeping?"

"Congratulations! I'm keeping well. Ryan and I have come home from France, we missed the English weather too much. We've bought a house in Hallingbury. How are

19

you finding your home? Can you believe it's almost been a year?"

"I can't, time seems to have flown by. I can't believe you're back in the UK, bet you're sad you sold the house now aren't you? Such a perfect family home."

"It is and I'm pleased I've bumped into you actually. This might all sound a little strange; it's something I wanted to tell you before we left the UK. Just something I think that you should know. A couple of years ago we decided to give the lounge a revamp, it was a little dated then and we were putting in a new fireplace. Anyway, when the builders were removing the old one, they came across something a little odd." Rachel said as she quickly glanced about the shop, checking that no-one was listening. "Behind the fireplace, so within the actual wall of the house, was a gravestone."

Yvonne stared into Rachel's eyes, half expecting her to start laughing, tell her that she was just fooling around but instead she continued,

"It was the gravestone of a little girl, Beth Robern. I know it must sound strange but we asked the builders to remove it so that we could store it in a safe place. Not because it scared us or made us feel uncomfortable but because we had such fond memories in that house that we knew if the time came and we moved, we wanted to take the gravestone with us. It could have been poor Beth who bought us luck and happiness all those years that we spent in your house."

Although Yvonne had been well acquainted with spirits and the paranormal, she came from a sceptical background and still found some things a little difficult to comprehend. "OK, I'm so shocked that there was a grave there in the first place, does anyone know why?" Yvonne asked as she put the book down that she was holding.

"No one knows, I guess it was collected and used in place of the bricks, perhaps by accident. We certainly never experienced anything untoward in the house. It has such a peaceful atmosphere. Do you agree?"

"I do," replied Yvonne, "I just hope that little Beth is still able to rest."

The women spoke a while longer before Rachel said her farewells and left Yvonne standing alone in the shop. *What a strange thing to tell me.* Yvonne thought as she tried to compose herself. The new information did not frighten her as much as she thought it would but it did when she thought about telling Eric. It had taken a lot to get him to move forward into a lighter future, away from the darkness of his former home in Poultney Road. Moving to the country had been the best thing that had happened to the pair of them and she did not want any more talk of ghosts.

Poultney Road was still owned by Flo. When her husband, Henry, had died, the house had been passed to her and because she suffered from senile dementia, Ellen was unable to sell the house on Flo's behalf which meant the two women still lived there; alone. Since Richard's death last year, Ellen often said how she longed to move to a smaller house without so many traumatic memories. Secretly, Ellen was terrified of 106 Poultney Road since Richard had died. Yvonne spoke to her every day and always ensured that she and Flo were doing fine. Ellen told her that the spirits Richard had bought into the house had not left. She would often hear familiar footsteps running across the landing, hear the cries of children and the laughter of men, but Yvonne wondered whether there was anything that Ellen chose to hold back from telling her. Since Richard's final séance, it seemed as though the most malevolent ghost had been banished. Yvonne hoped that whoever the man in black was that he was finally able to rest in peace, but she doubted so. She often thought of Ellen and Flo, alone in that house. Ellen had plenty of friends in the area, so she knew that she could call upon someone closer if she needed them. Yvonne worried that something might happen, and if it did, she would not be able to get to her in time.

"Everything OK Eve?" Ron asked. He was the owner of the shop and also a neighbour of Yvonne's.

"Sorry, yes. Everything's fine. I'll just take these." She handed him a couple of magazines from the display.

She left the shop and made her way back to her little red Mazda. Eric had always chosen Yvonne's cars so it was lucky he had good taste. She sat still and alone in the driver's seat for five or ten minutes. She did not know how long. She was deep in thought; much about the gravestone that had been taken from her home. She decided to visit the town library to see what history she could find on Greenmay Close.

*****

She was not a regular visitor in the library, but she knew her way around after several years of taking Jane. She was greeted by a softly spoken librarian who sent her in the right direction to find snippets and research on local history as well as the library's obituaries. She trailed through stories about local politics, missing people and much of the same until she came across a small article written in the local paper in 1946 about a fire on a pig farm on the East side of the town. Could this be what Yvonne was looking for?

Eleven people died, including eight children who were sleeping in their beds. People reported hearing screams around nine o'clock. They arrived as fast as they could but were unable to get anywhere close to the scene as the flames devoured the small farm. The victims are yet to be identified.

Yvonne took the clipping downstairs and over to the front desk where the petite librarian was standing.

"Can I help?" she asked?

22

"You can," replied Yvonne, eyes gleaming with anticipation. "I've just come across this article in the history section and it describes a fire that started in Sawbridgeworth. It was around the mid-forties. The article claims it took several lives on a small farm in the town. Do you have any idea where the farm would have been?"

"I'm afraid not," the young woman replied sadly, "I haven't lived round here long, but perhaps if you come back during the week, another Librarian might be able to help you."

Yvonne smiled briefly at her as she turned away, the disappointment showing on her face.

"Excuse me," came a soft voice from the other side of the room. "I'm sorry to intrude on your conversation but I couldn't help but overhear you asking about the fire in the forties."

"That's right," Yvonne replied as she made her way over towards the mysterious voice.

Welcoming her on the other side of the aisle was a lady no taller than five foot, with thinning grey hair and skin so wrinkled it would challenge a prune. All the same, she had the most delicate features and striking green eyes that Yvonne had ever seen.

"I've lived in these parts for almost eighty years and never has there been a fire so catastrophic. Those poor children." The lady said as her throat choked and she lowered her eyes to her feet. Yvonne noticed that the elderly woman was clenching her hand into a tight fist, pushing her nails hard into the skin. The frail woman looked drowned in devastation as though she had been hit by a thousand memories. "My name's Edith. Edith Riding."

The elderly woman continued to explain how no one had ever learned the cause of the fire. "Several people died, including my best friend, Mable. Her husband worked on the farm and they were given a home there so he could work early mornings. She was found in the same room as her children who also died from inhaling the smoke fumes. We think she tried to save them, but we can never be sure. Why is it you were asking dear? Do you live locally?"

"I do. My family and I have recently moved into the town and I like to know a bit of history about the place we're living."

"Well the fire was close to Valients Road, over by Greenmay Close. When they cleared everything up from the fire, there was nothing left. The cattle, pigs and horses they kept there all died or escaped. They didn't build anything on the land for a few years but I think that there are some nice houses over there now."

"That's where I live," Yvonne said; her brain processing the information. "Greenmay Close! Do you know where they buried the bodies?"

"I don't know for certain. They kept everything quite hush and I wasn't even invited to the funeral." Edith explained with a grimace. "Mable was my best friend, and to this day I don't know where she was buried. I presumed she was laid to rest in the cemetery next to the church in town but I never found her gravestone there."

"OK, well it's been lovely talking to you and thank you so much for your time and information but I need to make my way home now." Yvonne said, "I hope to see you around the town."

She shook the woman's hand and took the paper back to its box, hidden away amongst hundreds of others. When she got home, she still had a few hours to kill before she had to collect Jane from school and decided to take her mind off of the information she'd learned and bake a chocolate sponge for the evening's dessert. *So much for following doctors' orders,* she thought.

Chapter Two. Never too early.

It was the weekend and Yvonne visited her parents who had recently moved to a bungalow in a quaint cul-de-sac in Epping. Like most other Saturdays, she was taking her Mother, Elsie, into town to help her get food for the week. She wrapped her arm gently around Elsie's back as they made their way into the butchers.

"What are you thinking of eating for dinner tonight Mum?" Yvonne asked as they made their way over to the counter, smiling at Arthur who awaited Elsie's request.

"Good morning Arthur, is your braising steak good today?" Elsie asked as she considered the meat in the display cupboard.

"Only the best for you," he replied as he dropped a wink at Yvonne.

"Then I'll have half a kilo, cut into cubes please and two pieces of kidney." Elsie said as she reached into her handbag for her purse.

She had been a customer of Arthur's for the best part of two years and even popped in sometimes when they had lived in Abridge. Elsie thanked him, made her way outside with Yvonne where they took their usual stroll down to the local café, Poppy's, for a bite to eat. They ordered and made themselves comfortable.

"Mum, why don't you and Dad believe in ghosts?" Yvonne asked as she hooked the loose strands of hair across her cheek behind her ear. "We've never really spoken about it before; you and Dad have always been religious and yet you don't believe in an afterlife."

Elsie sat for a moment. "What an odd thing to ask. Is everything OK?"

Yvonne looked down, not wanting to make eye contact and avoiding any further interrogation. "It is, I'm just curious."

"I don't really know love; I guess we've never experienced anything of the sort. I know that there must be something after death, but I'm not sure what I believe if I'm honest. I haven't ever really had to think about it," she looked at her daughter. "Are you sure everything's alright?"

Yvonne went to reply but the waitress came over with their food. The interruption was probably a Godsend. Although Yvonne was tempted to explain the experiences she had when she first met Eric and the discovery of the gravestone in her house; it was probably best kept unsaid.

"Yvonne?" Elsie retorted.

"No, Mum, everything's fine. Let's eat."

*****

Yvonne decided not to tell her family about her earlier encounter with Rachel, or the woman she had met in the library. It probably didn't mean anything and would cause unnecessary aggravation. Eric would most likely dismiss the information anyway; growing up with such an insight into the paranormal left him a hard person to scare. The weeks passed, and Yvonne felt the baby inside her grow bigger and more active every day. On the 6th October 1983, she still had another four weeks before she met her little bundle and was bursting with excitement.

"Can I go round Stacey's house tonight, Mum? There are a few girls going over." Jane whined.

"OK, but your Dad will have to take you. I'm exhausted," she said, resting her elbow on the side board and her head in the palm of her hand, "so you need to go grovel to him."

Jane didn't hang about and ran from the kitchen to the lounge where her Dad was watching football. No sooner had she begged, did Yvonne hear the clatter of car keys and a call from the hall, "I won't be ten minutes, just dropping Jane round her friends."

The front door opened and then closed behind them. Yvonne was preparing homemade cottage pie but craved a big juicy steak. The temptation of tender meat, oozing with rareness had her dribbling at the thought, but she reminded herself that baby would not appreciate such tastes. The smell of rich gravy filled the room and she was temporarily transported back to her childhood when Elsie would cook the same meal for her and her brother, Ben. Adolescent thoughts flowed as she reminisced on her younger years.

Only a few minutes had passed when she heard him.

"Yvonne!" came a voice in the hallway, not far from where she was standing, "Yvonne, come quick!" The voice called.

For a moment she thought it was Eric, perhaps he had forgotten something or Jane had changed her mind, but as she ran passed the glass patio doors in the dining room, she could see that his car was not on the drive. Making it to the hall, she threw the light switch, opening her eyes to an empty space. Eric's shoes were not where he usually left them; his jacket had been taken from where it had been hanging on the cupboard. The house was empty.

"Hello?" She called, hoping that someone might answer. "Eric? Jane?"

She felt her hands tremble around the sharpened vegetable knife she was holding and her knees reciprocated the motion. She slowly backed herself towards the front door, eager to be close to an exit or escape should anything happen before her husband got home.

It was as she felt the cold of the glass door through her knitted, grey jumper that she was riddled with pain. It tightened throughout her lower abdomen, contracting in waves that travelled through her stomach and stabbed into her back.

"Eric!" she wailed, but no one was home; no one could hear her cries.

She dropped to her knees, as the painful spasms lingered like an involuntary nervous system had possessed her internal organs. *It can't be labour, I'm four weeks early,* she reassured herself and as she did, the pain eased, allowing her to stand and make her way into the lounge to the nearest phone.

999 she dialed.

"An ambulance please, I think I'm in labour.

*****

When Eric arrived home, less than fifteen minutes later, blue lights were flashing outside his house. He darted from the car to the front door, his feet barely touching the ground. Calling out to his wife as he dashed in to the hallway, he saw her being lifted into a wheelchair.

"Mr Camp?" A stocky man in his late forties asked.

Eric nodded.

"Your wife is in labour, we need to get her to the hospital right away," the man explained. "As you know, she's more than a month early and it's important we get her seen by a doctor as soon as possible."

Again, Eric nodded, this time making his way over to his wife.

"She's going to be fine, she's in safe hands," the ambulance driver reassured.

*****

More than twelve hours later, Stephanie was born at nine o clock in the morning. Both Mother and baby were fine and perfectly healthy. Eric had gotten hold of Stacey's Mum and suggested that Jane stay there for the next day or two but Jane wasn't having any of it, she wanted to meet her

28

baby sister immediately and asked Stacey's mum to drop
her at the hospital.

*****

By the time Jane arrived, Mervyn and Elsie were at
Yvonne's bedside. Her heart raced at the thought of
meeting her baby sister. As she made her way into the
maternity ward, she spotted her mother. Although weak and
extremely tired, she could sense the overwhelming pride
she showed on her face when she was able to introduce her
two daughters.

The birth had not been easy. Stephanie had been born
breach and at one point, Yvonne thought she might lose her
child. Eric had been sent out of the birth room as both baby
and Mum had gone into distress. Doctors had to use force
and introduce forceps to the birth, causing very sore
looking red veins to surface on Stephanie's ear and nose;
they had literally pulled at every orifice to get the baby out
whilst she was still breathing.

Jane kissed and greeted her parents and Grandparents,
and then turned to analyse her baby sister. Stephanie was in
a small, contained cot that Eric was watching over. She was
dressed in a small white baby-grow that swamped her tiny
body. Yvonne had explained that the incubator was to keep
her healthy whilst her body caught up with the weeks she
should have spent growing, cocooned in her mother's
womb. As Jane's eyes examined her minuscule body, she
could see that she may have been small but she was
perfectly formed. Jane walked to the right side of the cot,
wanting a closer look. Stephanie was wide awake but did
not make a sound. As Jane walked to face her, she was
instantly taken aback by the baby's bright blue eyes that
sparkled a glistening shade of purple.

"She's just perfect, Mum. Can I hold her?" Jane asked as she slid her finger across the outside of the glass that separated her from her sister.

"Not just yet, we need to make sure she's strong enough to fight infection first," Elsie said as she stood to hold her granddaughter's hand, "as soon as she's ready, you'll be able to cuddle and squeeze her as much as you like." She explained as she gently kissed Jane's forehead.

"Can you take Jane tonight, Dad? That way Eric can stay with us for a while."

"Of course," Mervyn replied, "would be our pleasure."

Before the three of them headed off, Ellen arrived with a cuddly bear tucked tightly beneath her right arm.

"Congratulations you two, where is she?" Ellen said as she bent down and kissed her son and daughter-in-law. She stumbled when Jane jumped up from her chair and hugged her tight, letting go only to grab her hand to lead her to the baby.

The family spent some time admiring Stephanie, but without being able to hold her it was hard to become over acquainted.

"I should let you both get some rest, you must be exhausted," Ellen said as she stood to her feet, wiping down the back of her skirt.

"I knew she would come early you know; I said it from the start." Yvonne uttered from the depths of her pillow, eyes closed as she drifted in and out of sleep. "I knew she would come today. It's Dick's birthday." Ellen and Eric exchanged glances, neither of them wanting to hold the gaze for too long; neither of them wanting to feel grief on such a celebratory day. "It's his way you know, it was his wish to tell me and now he has. Happy birthday, Dick." Yvonne continued before drifting into a deeper sleep, leaving her husband, parent's, Jane and Ellen all looking into the glass cot at the Camp's new edition.

*****

When Yvonne woke the next morning, the sun shone bright through the gap in the curtain, resting its rays down on her new born baby's head. Eric was asleep in the chair at the end of the bed, his hair messed and clothes creased. He must have done the night shift and she knew she should make the most of it; he had never done them with Jane so he was unlikely to carry on once they got home. Holding her stomach as she stood, her insides were still tender as she pulled herself to her feet.

"Morning beautiful," she whispered to her tiny baby, and lifted her slowly into her arms. Her skin felt as soft as silk as she stroked her plump little cheeks. She inhaled that somewhat unfamiliar smell that a baby has; a sweet, musky aroma that sent Yvonne's senses into another dimension. The bond was instant; she spent twenty minutes lying with her bundle of baby on her chest, gazing at her, watching her sleep. She may have been born early, but Yvonne knew that this little one was going to be a fighter.

Chapter three. The right way.

The first six months of Stephanie's life flew by. Her body filled out, knees dimpled and hair grew; the violet in her eyes deepened and her smile was permanent. She was a happy baby and bought joy to the Camp household; give or take a few sleepless nights. Yvonne knew how important it was to have her parents and Ellen in her daughter's life, and they would often look after the girls when Yvonne and Eric went away for business or treated themselves to a date night.

The same as they did with Jane, they decided to have Stephanie christened. They were not practising Christians but both parents had faith. They set the date for May 3rd 1984 and invited their closest friends and family. The morning of the Christening, Elsie arrived at Greenmay Close early to help Yvonne set up. Yvonne wore a cute plaid two-piece, bright red and fitted, and a little jacket trimmed with a delicate lace collar. Elsie was wearing a tiny beige suite that covered her petite frame. Both women were rummaging their way about the kitchen, like caterers preparing for an annual banquet.

Eric came down the stairs smartly finished in his brown smock suit, thick black hair swept over to one side, looking bang-on trend.

"You girls look a picture," Eric said as he came into the kitchen. "Where's Mervyn?" His attention was on the buffet that was being laid out around him.

"Hands off!" Yvonne said, smacking his greedy hand away from the sausage rolls. "He's meeting us at the church, we'll be taking Mum with us," she replied, covering the sandwiches with film and setting them in the fridge ready for later.

Yvonne had dressed Stephanie in a long, over-the-top lace gown with matching bonnet.

"Where's Jane?" Elsie asked, half-knowing the answer.

"Two guesses," Yvonne replied. "Go call her, Eric, we need to leave in five minutes."

Eric made his way out of the kitchen, "Don't forget your camera." Yvonne called after him.

At Jane's christening, they had been lucky enough that Richard, Eric's Dad, offered to photograph the day. He always had the best equipment and, being a professional, they always took advantage. Photography was a way of life for him and had been ever since he was a teenager. He had always said that *there's nothing a photo can't capture,* and he was right. It was such a shame that he was missing such a special day. How proud he would have been to be a granddad to another little girl. Yvonne knew however, that he would be there in spirit.

Jane came gliding into the room. She had rummaged through Elsie's wardrobe, with permission of course, and found a beautiful cashmere suit. It was a neutral colour, pulled together by large, wooden buttons. The jacket was so petite that it was the perfect size for Jane who was only thirteen. It sat above the high-waisted skirt and neatly covered the cream, silk blouse she wore beneath it.

"Jane you look beautiful," Yvonne said as she made her way over to her daughter and gently kissed her forehead. "Have you thanked Nanny for letting you wear her best suit?"

"Of course I have, thank you Nanny." She replied, throwing her arms around her Nan's tiny waist.

One-by-one they all made their way outside and to Eric's Jaguar. Jane and Elsie elected themselves to sit in the back with Steph. They made it to the church just as a few of the guests started to arrive. Amongst the small gathering, Yvonne spotted Pip and Ken, Stephanie's godparents-to-be. Shaking hands and greeting others as she passed them carrying Stephanie, the main attraction, it was like wading through a crowd with a puppy, everyone wants to stop you for a look.

"Pip, you look stunning," Yvonne said as she kissed the striking looking woman on the cheek, "and Ken, you don't scrub up too badly either,"

"Oh, thank you very much!" Ken replied, trying to hide the smile on his face. "And don't you look beautiful," he said to Stephanie who was sweetly cooing in her mother's arms.

"Do you mind holding her whilst I go and meet and greet?" Yvonne asked, handing the baby to Pip.

"What are Godparents for?" Pip said, tickling Steph's cheek.

"Thank you," she smiled before dashing off and doing the rounds.

Pip and Ken had a child of their own, a little boy a few years younger than Jane. They would have loved to have had a daughter to keep him company, but work commitments and the travelling it induced would not allow it. Being one of Yvonne and Eric's closest friends, they had decided—after much consideration—that they would be the perfect, compassionate and caring godparents for their little girl.

They all made their way into the church on the bright Sunday morning and proceeded to make their promises to Stephanie in the eyes of God. Baby kicked up a bit of a fuss when she was handed to the Priest and doused with water, but nothing out of the ordinary. Everyone said what a wonderful ceremony it was and after Eric took a few photos outside the church, they all made their way back to Greenmay Close where the celebrations commenced.

Back at the after party everyone took their turn holding Steph, complimenting in the usual way; *hasn't she got the most beautiful eyes, are they violet?* People asked. *Doesn't she look like you,* others proclaimed. Yvonne and Eric were doting parents and enjoyed the compliments and after offering their farewells to their guests, they enjoyed an evening with close family.

*****

The following weekend's weather was not quite as glorious. Although temperatures were still fairly high for that time of year, the heavens had opened and the rain had been falling in the early hours of the morning. Eric had promised Yvonne that he would take the camera film from the christening to the local developer. He looked outside the window upon waking and shivered as he watched the branches of the trees blow as the wind belted them like a cane to a school boys arse.

"They say the weather's only going to get worse," Eric told Yvonne as he pulled the curtains together and walked back over to their bed where his wife was lying, still tucked in and wrapped up tight.

It was early, about seven o'clock, around the time that Stephanie normally woke, crying for her parents' attention which would often result in Jane screaming from her bedroom for them to silence her. This morning, no one was yelling and Yvonne was enjoying the peace.

"Check on Steph," she asked Eric who was about to climb back into bed, "it's odd for her to still be sleeping."

Huffing and making his frustration obvious, Eric grabbed a t-shirt from the back of Yvonne's dresser stool, knocking a bottle of Chanel perfume flying through the air and on to the floor. Yvonne saw him eye the bottle and walk on past, obviously wanting to prove some kind of point. She squinted her eyes to watch her husband's annoyance but it only amused her. It was rare she asked him to do anything around the house or for the children so she was making damn sure she did not move on this occasion. A few moments passed before Eric came back into the room holding Stephanie, who was wide awake and giggling in her father's arms.

36

"She was awake when I went in there," Eric said as he tickled his daughter's bare arm. "She was sitting up in her cot, cooing, strangely, at the far wall," he said as he perched Stephanie next to Yvonne before climbing into bed beside them.

"We're lucky she knows how to amuse herself," Yvonne quirked as she pushed herself up and faced her daughter who was now tugging slightly on her mother's hair as it fell across her face.

Yvonne looked into Stephanie's violet eyes as they pierced through her own. She remembered back to when Jane was the same, dependant age and a tear filled her eye. *Time always passes too fast,* she thought as she felt Eric's arm wrap around her leg.

"What are you thinking? You look lost," he asked.

"Nothing really, just of how lucky we are," she smiled as she laid her head back down and let it deepen within the pillow.

*****

It was around ten o'clock that Eric left for town. He would usually play football on a Saturday; he played for and managed a team called Audwelli Wanderers, put together by Eric and consisting of his best friends, work acquaintances and other men who he had met and talked into getting involved. The team probably took it too seriously but they loved it, and Yvonne played her part too. She was responsible for preparing the half-time oranges and washing the sweat-filled kits after a game, a delightful addition to her weekend chores which most of her friends told her to refuse, but in fact she secretly enjoyed it. Today the game had been cancelled due to the adverse weather conditions. The rain had not stopped all night and the pitch was flooded, which was enough to put Eric in a bad mood from the start.

He had no intention of being long in town. He absolutely hated shopping and was simply fulfilling the promise he made to his wife to get the photos from the christening developed. The hour they took to develop he intended to walk to the nearest coffee shop and treat himself to a pastry. He rubbed down the stretch of his stomach and felt the gentle ripple of muscle. He had worked out at the gym all week so he felt he deserved the treat. *All work and no play*, he thought.

He turned into the car park that was behind a large chemist in town, the indication sound was drummed out by the hammering of the rain on his windscreen.

"Shitty weather," he cursed as he pulled into a space. The weather often had an effect on the availability of spaces to park and there were plenty of spaces that miserable May morning. *Well there's one good thing,* he told himself.

He grabbed his wallet from the passenger's seat and got himself a two hour ticket which he stuck to the inside of his windscreen as his hair stuck to the dampness of his face. He grabbed a loose copy of the Daily Mirror which had been on the parcel shelf for at least two weeks. The football player and his fancy woman pictured on the cover settled against his head, protecting it from the downpour.

He pushed through the doors of Developing Stages and headed straight over to the counter. The woman who greeted him was tall, slender with a lot of eye makeup and back-combed hair sitting on the top of her head. She reminded him a lot of the lead singer of his favourite rock band, but he failed to recall the name.

"Good morning, Sir. Can I help you?" asked the lady's polite tone.

"Yes please, I'd like this film developed today. Within the hour would be great," he asked as he handed over the film.

"This service isn't yet available sir, the minimum time in which we can develop a film is twenty-four hours," she informed with a huge grin on her face, "want me to book it in?" she asked.

Eric's face crumpled, "I guess you'll have too. Will they be ready Monday afternoon? I take it you aren't open on Sundays," he asked, trying to take his mind off of the fact that he had just wasted almost a pound on parking. "So a forty-eight service, not twenty-four like you're saying?"

"They will be ready Monday, Sir, yes," she answered, still with the same sarcastic smile.

"See you then," he replied as he slammed the door of the shop closed behind him.

*****

Monday soon came and checking the clock on the wall, Eric informed his business partner, Ryan, of his *chore* and that he had needed to head home at three o'clock to ensure he got to the shop in time before closing. The business had moved to Bethnal Green, a central location close to the London taxi trade that the company worked on; the journey home to Hertfordshire would take at least forty-five minutes.

Eric had started Wolfelec Limited when he had enough of working on his market stall. He manufactured and fitted all manner of accessories to the black cab and business was positively booming. He arrived at the shop around four o'clock and parked in the same car park as before. This time he had to drive around looking for a space for ten minutes before he saw a man, in no hurry, walking back to his banged-up Ford Escort, which was parked at the rear end of the car park. Beating an elderly woman to the space, Eric felt no shame and made his way to the shop.

As he pushed through the pokey door, the familiar bell rung, this time as he made his way to the counter there was

39

a man who greeted him; possibly the owner. He wore a name badge on his discoloured white shirt that read, Jim. He was a short, stocky fella, with an emphasised comb-over and moustache that made him look like one of the musketeers.

"Hi, I've come to collect some photos I bought in on Saturday." Eric said as he handed him his docket.

"Thank you, Sir, I'll just go and get this for you."

Whilst the man disappeared out back, Eric let his eyes wander the walls where there were family photos hung, wedding day smiles and baby's dressed in ludicrous outfits whilst their parents smothered them adoringly. He smiled at the memory when, last month, Yvonne had talked him into joining his own family at a professional photo-shoot. He had spent the day previous coming down with man-flu and any other likely disease that he could think of to get out of it but his wife got her own way in the end. Jane enjoyed the opportunity to get dolled up and Yvonne simply loved the family time. He was pleased afterwards that he had backed down and actually enjoyed himself.

"OK, here we are," the man walked back into the shop through the beaded curtains that seemed to be becoming quite popular recently. "We have two sets of prints here for you Mr Camp," the man continued as he placed down two pocket wallets containing photographs.

"No, no, you must be mistaken, I only bought one set in to be developed," Eric replied whilst taking his wallet from his black-leather jacket pocket, "unless my wife bought them in before?"

The man looked at Eric. "It's odd you should say that, as the second development doesn't appear to have been done here, they haven't got the Kodak markings on the back of them and neither do they have our protective wallet," the man said as he lifted the prints and handed them to Eric. "Take a look at them and check to see if they're yours. I won't charge you either way as I'm not sure where they've come from."

Eric took the photos and instantly recognised the brown paper wallet that they were in. He carefully pulled back the envelope and lifted out the set of prints.

"Impossible." Eric stood in front of Jim as he flicked through every photograph in the set. "And you're sure you don't know where these came from?" Eric asked, his face turning pale.

"Definitely not, they look like home developed photos to me."

Eric stamped a tenner on the counter, grabbed the second set of prints and made his way out of the shop without waiting for his change. His feet could not take him fast enough as he scurried his way through the pushchairs and whining children, back to the car park where his car sat waiting for him. He was aware his foot was pressed too hard on the accelerator but needed to get home to his wife as soon as he could. Maybe she could make some sense of it.

He pulled his car onto the drive, next to his wife's convertible and threw the door closed behind him. His hands were trembling as he pushed the key into the lock,

"Yvonne, you need to come see this." He called as he made his way into the house searching for his wife. "Yvonne!" He yelled this time, as he felt his patience wither.

"Calm down, I'm here. What's the drama?"

Eric passed Yvonne the brown wallet.

"What's this?" she asked as she lifted out the photographs but her expression soon changed as she realised why her husband was behaving so strangely.

For a moment, neither of them said a word. Yvonne made her way from the hall into the lounge and felt her way to seat herself on the sofa, her eyes never distracting from the images in front of her.

41

She looked up to meet Eric's gaze, "Where did you get these?"

"I'm right aren't I? I'm right in thinking that these photos never got developed?"

Yvonne's attention returned to the photos she was holding in her hand. The one which sat on top was of her and Ellen, sitting in the lounge of the home she owned in Poultney Road, opposite to where Eric had grown up. She recognised the setting and what they were celebrating immediately as it was the only time she had ever worn that electric blue suit. The next photo was of Jane, seven months old and wearing her christening gown. Every photo had been taken at Jane's christening, thirteen years ago. One person missing from the photo was Richard. He was missing because he had been the only one that day to take any pictures. It was his gift to them that he wanted to give them in a baby album but the day after Jane's christening, when Richard had gone to develop the film; it had been exposed to sunlight and every image had been destroyed. They had never seen any photos from that day.

"How?" Yvonne asked as tears filled her eyes. "How is this possible?"

Chapter Four. Fall.

Ellen had given up her job at the local launderette and had started to work for Eric's company at Wolfelec Ltd. It seemed at one time or another, every member of the Camp family worked for Eric; he always managed to find something for someone who needed the cash. Ellen had been working two jobs and what with looking after Flo, it had become too difficult for her to cope. She was only in her sixties but was drained, physically and mentally. Eric needed an extra pair of hands, to put kits together and tidy up any loose ends. It was something that Ellen could do from home; enabling her to keep an eye on Flo so that she did not wander into town or give away anymore of her jewellery to passers-by (which she had been known to do).

It had been a day that had started off so well; Ellen had made them breakfast and Flo actually ate; a rare occurrence as more often than not Flo would think she was too busy or simply refuse to eat altogether. That day, however, Ellen had managed to get Flo to eat at the breakfast table and finish up all of the toast that she had spread with marmalade for her. She did not have any work from Eric, so she suggested that once they were both dressed, they would take a walk into town and see her good friend and ex-boss, Barbara, who owned the laundrette. Ellen knew all too well that Flo had been taking longer than usual to get dressed, but she decided to leave her for a little while as she thought perhaps she was getting dolled up, which she had taken to doing. She enjoyed that.

Ellen moved about the kitchen, sorting through cupboards and drawers that she had not looked in for some time, certainly not since Richard's death. She never dealt with grief well—a trait which had passed down to her three sons, they all chose to keep things bottled up. She had not sorted through any of Richard's belongings, though both

Yvonne and Janet nagged her about it often. Instead, she had simply boxed it all up and put it in the attic for safe keeping, perhaps for the same reason why she had not gone through the communal cupboards. She did not want to open any more memories because memories caused pain. *Best keep it locked up*, she thought as she semi-opened the kitchenette drawer, almost tempted by the curiosity that was niggling away at her.

Ellen's thought process was interrupted by the sound of footsteps overhead, from Flo's bedroom to the middle of the landing by the top of the stairs. Ellen paused momentarily, silencing her movement to see if she could hear anything else. She knew that it could not be Flo; she was ninety-eight years old and if she could move as quick as that then she should own a place in the *Guinness Book of Records*.

"Mum?" Ellen called down the hall, as she turned to face the direction of the stairs.

She felt a chill run through her as her skin prickled with the cool breeze that blew through the room. She looked down at her bare arms and saw that every hair there was stood on end, the same as it had so many times before; so many dark memories hiding in her thoughts, hidden within the four walls of the house.

Her daydream was interrupted by a thud directly above her, "Mum!" She yelled this time, not able to move her feet fast enough, almost slipping on the lino floor that was still moist from the clean it had that morning.

What came next would haunt Ellen for years, possibly her entire life. Flo screamed, so close but too far away for Ellen to be able to protect her, to save her from whatever was in the house with them. As Ellen almost reached the bottom of the stairs, she heard a sound from Flo that was hard to decipher. It was something similar to the retch of someone about to vomit but wholehearted trying to scream or cry out simultaneously. Seconds later Ellen heard her

44

fall, one step, two, three; Flo fell the full flight of the stairs—top to bottom—and by the sounds of it, she must have hit every one of them. Ellen met her at the final step and cushioned her landing but sadly not preventing the injuries that she had already incurred.

"Mum, what happened? What the hell has happened?" Ellen cried, trying hard to cover the fear that lingered in her voice; tears streaming from her eyes and soaking her mother-in-law's fine, grey hair. "Mum, I'll get you an ambulance, hold on for me. Hold on."

*****

Her somber mood was rivalled by the brightly lit waiting room which stunk of vomit infused bleach. Ellen had been waiting for what seemed like hours before Yvonne and Eric arrived. She could not comfort herself whether she was standing and pacing the dismal corridors or sitting still on one of the dirty, plastic chairs; nothing could help pass the minutes quick enough that she could forget the events that had happened that morning. Her thoughts filled briefly with images of her mother-in-laws face, frozen still with fear impressed upon every orifice. Her eyes wide, glazed like an animal in headlights, fearful for its life; her mouth pried open by the rigidness of her jaw. What had she seen? Who or what had been upstairs with her, scaring the living hell out of an elderly women? She may not have had a heart attack but Ellen knew that her state of mind would be further damaged by the trauma.

"Ellen!" She instantly recognised the comforting sound of her daughter-in-laws voice, calling her from the far side of the waiting room, "We came as fast as we could. Eric is just parking the car," Yvonne said as she threw her arms around Ellen's neck, steadying her from toppling over; her knees still trembling. "Whatever happened?"

45

Ellen began to explain the events as they unfolded inside 106 Poultney Road. The pleasant breakfast they had shared, Flo going upstairs alone to get changed for their shopping trip in town and then, "I heard footsteps, Yvonne." Ellen said, her eyes welling full, "I thought this had all stopped when Richard…" she paused before she could bring herself to say the word, "died. I thought they had left us alone, left me alone but they haven't."

Yvonne sat Ellen down on a hospital chair which had a very slight padding on the seat, almost a blessing compared to those nasty hard plastic ones.

"How do you know that it wasn't Flo you heard, Ellen? How do you know that she wasn't walking around the landing and simply tripped?"

"Because she can't run," Ellen said, looking her daughter-in-law directly in the eye. "I heard someone running up there, and then I heard her scream," Ellen began to sob, "I can't do this Yvonne, I can do this without Richard."

Eric came running through the double glass doors to find his wife cradling his mother's head in her arms. He caught Yvonne's eye as she used her free hand to call him over. Before he reached his family, a doctor began to approach them from the far end of the corridor, behind where Ellen and Yvonne were sitting. He was a tall, slim man, probably in his mid-forties, dark hair and dressed in the usual white outfit; clearly confident at giving relatives news on his patients. Yvonne spotted him as she followed her husband's gaze, "Doctor, how is she?" She asked before he had time to make it all the way over to them, "is she conscious?"

"Hello," he said, in a very calm voice, ignoring Yvonne's concern, "My name is Dr Franklin. I am looking after your mother. Flo is awake, I have just spoken to her but she isn't yet coherent about the events which took place this morning and I don't particularly want her poached too

46

soon. It could cause further confusion. Who was it that was with her?"

"It was me," Ellen said, clearing her throat, "I was in the house when it happened. Is she going to be OK?"

"She's going to be fine. We just need to determine whether her fall was a cause of her illness or whether it was simply a case of misjudgement when she's come to walk down the stairs," Dr Franklin explained. "Now, tell me, was it only the two of you alone inside the house at the time of the accident?" He asked.

"Yes," Ellen replied, wiping the tears that dwelled in the corners of her eyes, creasing her brow slightly, confused where the question was leading.

"Sorry, let me explain. Like I said, Flo has only just woken up, she does seem a little disorientated but all she keeps saying is that someone pushed her down the stairs."

Ellen's face frowned even more, bewildered at the doctor's suggestive tone. "You think I pushed my elderly mother-in-law down a flight of stairs? Is that what you're trying to say?"

"I'm not saying anything of the sort Mrs Camp, but what I am suggesting is that your mother's fall was due to a hallucination bought on by her Alzheimer's disease. Obviously we will need to speak to her once she has calmed down, but I think it may be sensible for you to consider having her looked after properly in a home. I think she needs twenty-four hour care. I'll leave it with you to think about it, but in the meantime please feel free to visit Flo, but try not to crowd her, like I say, she is still a little disorientated."

The Camp's followed Dr Franklin into Flo's hospital room which was crowded with five more elderly patients, all women and all fed with drips and coated in bruises. Flo was at the back of the room, her injuries looked worse than the other women's. Her face was almost entirely purple, the same shade that a banana turns when its bruised and over-

47

ripe, with dark patches spread across a pale surface, you could barely see her eyes hidden beneath their swollen pockets. She looked as though she had been involved in a car accident, never mind a mere fall down a flight of stairs.

"Nan!" Eric proclaimed as he made his way over to Flo, who did not so much as acknowledge his arrival.

"Whatever happened?" he asked, taking her tiny, cold hand into his.

Flo slowly moved her head round to face them, passed Eric who was kneeling by her bedside, Yvonne who had seated herself on the bottom of her bed, straightening out the sheets, and looked at Ellen, "She did this to me," Flo said, throwing out her accusation, "she pushed me down the stairs. Help!" Flo screamed, "Help me!" she continued to call.

"Nan!" Eric said who was desperate to calm his Nan down.

"They know what you did, Ellen; they know and they'll punish you," and without another word, Flo rested her head back onto her pillow, closed her eyes and fell back into a deep sleep before Dr Franklin even had chance to respond to the screams.

*****

Yvonne and Eric dropped Ellen home. Seeing what a state she had gotten herself into, they offered for her to spend the night with them, but she was adamant that she wanted to be alone. And who would blame her for feeling so distraught. Eric could not understand why she would want to further her punishment by being alone but he did not continue to nag his mother, although Yvonne would have liked him to be a little more persuasive.

Pulling up outside the familiar house on Poultney Road, Yvonne looked up at its full glory. The paintwork was worn around the window sills and the brickwork could have done with a clean.

"Shall I come over tomorrow, Ellen? It's such a big house to keep clean by yourself. I'll give you a hand?" Ellen did not move nor answer for a moment; her eyes were transfixed upon the front window. Yvonne followed her gaze, "Steph would love to see you. It'll be a real adventure for her; I'll bring some lunch?"

The window was empty but Ellen had lost herself within it for a moment, "sorry Eve, yes that sounds lovely, so long as you don't mind." It was a statement rather than a question and she climbed out of the car and thanked them both for the lift.

"Are you positive you don't want us to come in, Mum?" Eric asked.

"I'm sure, I just want to have some dinner and lose myself in a Mills and Boon for the rest of the evening." *Hopefully Flo's screams won't follow me into the lustrous pages*, she thought. "Safe journey home," she called from the front door, stepping inside and closing the barrier between her and the outside world.

She made it only as far as the front room, the one which had once, not many years before, belonged to her two youngest boys. Time past by so fast, too quickly to appreciate what you have and what could be so easily lost. She leant her back against the wall behind her, the coldness of the brick forcing its way through her chiffon blouse and onto her skin, raising goose-bumps along the surface, prickling the hairs that sat there.

"Ellen," she heard a voice calling her from upstairs, "Ellen, I need you," the voice said, pleading with her.

Ellen sat still for a moment, holding her own breath, anticipating what was going to come next. The voice sounded somewhat familiar, it was clearly a woman because she was comforted by her tones. Ellen wiped her eyes dry on the back of her hand, tasting the salt as tears fell loose upon her cheek. Pushing herself up, her body felt heavy, her knees bent as her legs almost gave way, causing her to lose balance. She grabbed a hold of the handle on the door beside her to steady herself.

"Ellen," the echoing accent called again, this time it sounded impatient.

Ellen had relaxed into a trance-like state that was only awakened when she was disturbed by a loud thud coming from above her head. She jumped up, bending her knees slightly, crouching into a more stable position and throwing up her hands to protect her head. Silence returned as she found the courage to straighten herself out and make her way to the bottom of the stairs. Above her, the upstairs landing was hiding in the darkness.

"Hello?" she called out. It was four o'clock in the afternoon and the sun was still high outside, but inside it could have been midnight. It was cold and dark, not even the windows allowed any sunlight through. No light resided there. "Hello? Who's there?"

As Ellen listened, she could hear the soft murmur of people talking, like a radio that was turned down so low that you had to strain to hear what they were saying but this was so quiet that no amount of silencing would make it audible. She left the light off, not wanting to disturb whatever, whoever it might be residing in the house. She took one step, then another up the staircase. Her third step made the boards creak and she paused momentarily, taking in a long, deep breath as she did. The conversation that was taking place alleviated but did not stop, so she continued on her way. She held firmly to the oak banister on her right and the dado rail to her left, using her arms to pull herself up, resisting what her head was telling her. She should run, she should run outside and scream for help. Call Robert who would surely be home and ask to stay there for the night. She knew that she should be doing anything but what she was doing. Over the years curiosity had lingered in her like a persistent cough you can't shift, attaching itself to her morbid curiosity. Richard had always protected her from the darkness he messed with; he had tried to shield her from seeing the things that had strengthened his beliefs. He had never given her credit for how strong her nerves were; that sometimes, she wanted to see with her own eyes. She wanted to know what was happening inside her home. Now that he was gone, she wanted to feed her hunger for curiosity; she wanted to know what her husband had done.

She took herself to the top of the staircase, pulling the buttons together on her thick cardigan as the air seemed to grow colder the further into the house she walked. It was clear to her that she could hear people talking, a soft murmur of conversation in the front bedroom behind the closed door. Nothing shocked her, she had lived through enough spooks and terrifying experiences to know that such paranormal phenomena existed, but facing it alone was a whole new ball game. She tip-toed across the landing, the worn carpet cushioned the balls of her feet. As she got closer, she hushed her breathing and concentrated on the voices from within the room. It sounded as though there were a group of at least five or six people. It was mainly a man speaking now, talking to whoever accompanied him. The man's voice was familiar.

"Repeat after me," he said, "if anyone's there give us a sign. Talk to us,"

Richard. The man who was speaking inside that room was Richard. *Impossible!* Ellen told herself, but she was done with listening, she could not contain her inquisitiveness any longer, she had to see what was happening inside the closed room. Was it possible that what she was hearing was her husband's spirit? If it was, then she was correct to believe that her husband's spirit was trapped in the property. *How could I ever leave,* she thought.

Her hand reached out for the door handle but she hesitated. She swallowed hard as she filled her lungs with fresh breath, before grabbing a hold of it. The cold brassiness of it made her flinch as it sent a bitter pulse of icy shock up her arm. She pushed down on the handle, the voices inside still chanting, "Give us a sign. Please give us a sign," they were calling in unison. She pushed hard into the door as it flung open, moving quicker than she had anticipated, causing her to misplace her footing and landing in a heap on the floor.

The room felt cold, really cold, and as she lifted her head to see only the bareness of the four walls, a wind gushed passed her, through her hair and blowing into her face. It was a pleasant contrast to the coldness that surrounded her; it was a warm breeze that she raised her head into so that she could experience the pleasure in its entirety. It lasted only a few moments but the effect lingered. Ellen did not move from the spot on the floor in the front bedroom. She stayed there all night, and in fact it was the first night that she had slept all the way through since Richard had passed away.

Chapter Five. 'Tis the season.

Neither Yvonne nor Eric told anyone about the photographs; it was something that they themselves found hard to believe or even understand. When surmising from a bystander's perspective, the photographs seemed to be an impossible wonder as only irrational explanations could answer the phenomenon. They both had their own presumptions and theories which they shared only between themselves. Since Flo's accident, Ellen distanced herself; she spent days at home, making wiring kits for Eric. She was probably the only person that Yvonne trusted enough to confide in with all of the strange things that had been happening to her and around the house, but Yvonne knew that the timing was not right. Ellen had enough to contend with.

The summer months came and went as they always do in England, with the sun overpowered by the onslaught of rain and bitterly cold winds that every year, seemed to come back around too soon.

Christmas was Yvonne's favourite time of year. It meant that she could spend time with her family, spend too much money and eat too much food. Eric had always been the Bah-Humbug of the family; he had been bought up by Ellen and Richard finding coal in his stocking as a boy and a roast dinner on the table only if he was lucky. Every year Yvonne wanted to show him what he had missed out on during his adolescence. The nostalgia of waking up on the bitter cold mornings and checking outside for snow was something Elsie had done with Yvonne from a young age in the weeks leading up to Christmas Eve.

It was Stephanie's second Christmas, and being that she was more aware of what was happening, Yvonne asked to have the whole family to her. Her brother Ben had declined the offer as he had prior arrangements with his own family, and Flo was still in hospital since her fall in September.

"What time's everyone getting here?" asked Jane, who was wearing a bright pink pair of nylon tights, black tutu, slouch jumper and some funky, aluminous leg warmers that she had got from her Santa sack that morning.

"In about an hour," Yvonne replied whilst juggling a multitude of vegetables ready to be chopped. "Be a good girl and take care of your sister for me until everyone gets here."

Jane made her way into the lounge where Stephanie was sitting in her playpen watching *Button Moon* on the television. She was a sprightly child and was happy entertaining herself. Catching sight of Jane as she entered the room, Steph moved her legs and arms in sporadic sequence.

"Ainee! Ainee!" she called out to her sister, thrusting her limbs and head to get her attention.

"Come on you," Jane said, reaching down to her sister, "want to come and play with your toys upstairs?" Jane asked and giving Steph no choice, she carried the child upstairs to her bedroom.

Eric was still getting ready in his room, no doubt he was working on his abs or some other muscular group he was adamant to improve. Being an older Dad, he challenged himself to look and feel as young as the other parents who were almost half his age.

Jane took her baby sister into her bedroom with the night-time glow worm that Santa had bought her that morning – or so she believed - closed the door and pulled out the phone she had stolen from the hook downstairs to call her best friend, Felicity.

Jane had the second largest room in the house which sat above the garage making it colder than the other rooms for much of the year; although she did not mind as it also meant she could play her music a little louder and get away

54

with it. It had a small room attached to it which Yvonne always intended to make into an en-suite but would wait until Jane was sixteen before doing so. For now, it remained a very large walk-in wardrobe. Stephanie loved to play inside there; even though she was still young, the small proximity of the room offered security and a space that Jane did not mind her messing up.

Jane opened the small door which lead into the cupboard room, and switched on the light.

"You'll be alright in here won't you Steph? I just need to speak to Auntie Flick, OK?" Jane asked rhetorically as she pulled the door closed behind her, picked up the receiver and dialed out. "Hi Felicity, merry Christmas," she called as the echo of her friend's voice belted down the phone.

The girls talked excitedly for ten minutes or so about the presents they had received that morning and their intentions at the Christmas party on the twenty-seventh of December. Felicity had been a best friend of Jane's since she started secondary school three years ago. They both loved fashion and celebrities and had a slight obsession with Madonna, just like every other teenage girl.

Jane sat up on the bed. Steph had stopped shouting and making the playful noises she had been a moment ago. A little concerned, Jane stood up and walked over to the door of the cupboard and opened it quickly. Her sister was fine, and was playing with her back to Jane.

"Are you OK?" Felicity asked. A moment passed. "Jane?"

"Can I call you back? Something just come up," she said as she ended the call.

Steph was still sitting in the same place, facing the back of the cupboard. Throwing the phone onto her bed, Jane stepped into the cupboard and bent down to lift her sister up, "Steph you cheeky monkey, what are you playing with?"

55

Steph turned to the sound of her sister's voice and, flailing her arms as a baby does, swung a knife past her face, missing it by only an inch or so. Avoiding the swipe, Jane panicked, fell over and yelled for her parents. Hearing the commotion, Eric burst into the room as Jane was down on the floor, searching for the weapon. Lifting Stephanie into her arms, she passed her to her father as she began to explain what had just happened. Desperate to find the evidence, she hunted on her hands and knees amongst the clothes and shoes that were a sign of the many wardrobe malfunctions Jane had. But the knife was nowhere to be seen.

"But it was here a minute ago," Jane said, puzzled, as her eyes rummaged through the small room which was scattered with a rainbow of clothes. "Why do you think I'm so freaked out?"

Yvonne came up to the room and after putting Steph back in her play pen, all three of them looked for the said weapon, but it was nowhere to be found. Jane had a pretty enviable imagination and so her parents put the situation down to that, even though Jane argued her case as well as a Lawyer might in court.

By one o'clock, everyone had arrived; Ellen, Elsie and Mervyn. They made a fuss of Stephanie and handed their presents to Jane for her to hide beneath the tree. As ever, Ellen flirted somewhat with Mervyn, but he pretended not to notice. Elsie made no comment as she trusted her husband and found Ellen's behavior comical whilst she busied herself in the kitchen with her daughter.

The day passed by and besides Jane sulking for the most part, it was a pretty successful Christmas that everyone enjoyed. Mervyn took Elsie home at around nine o'clock as Ellen had decided to stay. Eric put Stephanie to bed, whilst Yvonne did the dishes. Ellen enjoyed the time off and sat watching useless comedy with Jane in the lounge.

56

"Nan, can I ask you something?" Jane said as she stood up and pushed the door to the lounge closed.

"Of course you can, anything my dear," Ellen said as she turned to face her Granddaughter who was now stood over by the far door.

Jane fidgeted as she found the words to say, "Do you believe in ghosts?"

No-one had ever asked Ellen that before and it took her by surprise. It made it worse that it was her fourteen year old Granddaughter who stood looking at her with such faith and trust, that Ellen felt like a teacher being asked by a student whether or not she smoked. She thought for a few moments but not long enough for Jane to acknowledge the pause.

"I believe that there's life after death, yes," she answered, eventually. "And I believe that there is enough evidence to suggest that although life ends at death, our souls continue to remain. So it depends on what you consider to be a ghost. Why do you ask anyway?"

Jane answered, playing nervously with the ring that she had perched on the tip of her index finger; a nervous habit she couldn't break.

"Today I'm certain that someone was in my bedroom with me and Steph. I felt their eyes on me, they felt close enough to touch if I could have seen them; it was like they were playing tricks with my mind." Jane's eyes began to fill and her vision blurred as she felt her Nan's arms wrap around her shoulders.

"It's OK, sweetheart, I believe you."

Her Nan's soothing words were enough to know the real answer to her question was, yes.

*****

Ellen stayed until midday on the twenty-seventh when she was dropped home, at the same time that Yvonne dropped Jane at Felicity's house around the corner.

"I'll come to pick you up tomorrow at eleven," Yvonne said as she kissed her daughter goodbye, "be ready for me."

"I will," Jane retorted as she made her way up the slightly overgrown driveway to her best friend's house.

The excitement overwhelmed her daughter's face, it was the first real party she was going to and Yvonne had bought her the dress that she had been looking at for months. Yvonne waved goodbye as she made her way back down the road, on her drive home. Eric was looking after Steph whilst Yvonne picked up some shopping from the local market. When she got home, Stephanie was asleep and Eric had his gym bag packed and settled on the bottom step.

"I'm meeting Peter at the gym, I'll only be gone an hour or two," Eric said as he tied the laces on his Reebok's. "I'm looking forward to it being just us tonight, I can bring a movie home if you like?"

"Great," replied Yvonne as she thought about jumping in a bath as soon as he left before Steph woke from her nap.

It was a rare occasion that she had any alone time and so she was planning on making the most of it. She reciprocated her husband's kiss and hastily made her way upstairs to the bathroom. They had a large bathroom with two sinks and a Jacuzzi-style tub she liked to relax in with magazines and a glass of something stronger than she would usually drink. Today was going to be one of those, rare yet special occasions when she got to do precisely that.

She ran the hot tap, closed the door behind her so that their new puppy, Holly, did not make any unwanted jumps in and scald herself. Yvonne shuddered at the thought. Holly was bought to be a companion to Steph as she grew up. They had always had a house full of pets and their previous dog, Sandy, had passed away a year ago and the home had felt empty without her. Jane liked animals but

58

she wasn't particular fussed when they had bought Holly home, she was more interested in boys.

Grabbing a Snowball, a glass and the copy of the Daily Mirror that had come through the door that morning, Yvonne made sure Holly was comfortable downstairs in the dining room and checked on Steph who was still sleeping in the room next to the bathroom. She placed the baby monitor on the floor next to the tub and undressed herself before stepping into the sweltering hot water. She felt her skin absorb the heat and as the perspiration intensified on her chin and forehead, she took a deep breath and a sip of what was her favourite tipple. Yvonne was never a big drinker, and since having her gallbladder removed, could manage only a glass of wine before giggling and setting off those around her in hysterics so her tastes had changed to Snowballs and Babychams.

Lost in a story about a woman who had caught her husband in bed with her best friend, Yvonne's attentions switched to the baby monitor that was sitting on the floor beside her. For the past five minutes she had been vaguely aware of her daughter breathing deeply, sleeping in amongst the silence that consumed the rest of the house. Suddenly the sound of breathing was accompanied by something else. A soothing humming sound emerged from behind the breathing. *Was someone else in there?* Yvonne placed the monitor against her ear as the humming abruptly stopped. There was something else there though, a faint noise that she could barely make out. It took her a moment before she recognised the sound; it was a child talking softly. She could hear Stephanie breathing but behind that there was the unmistakable sound of a child's laughter. Before Yvonne could respond, the faint noise rose in volume, and she heard child's footsteps running out of her daughter's bedroom, passed the bathroom and along the hall as the giggling echoed through the house.

Yvonne threw down the monitor and launched herself out of the bath, her skin enflamed by the heat of the water, feet soaking and slipping from the dampness as she directed herself across the slippery tiles of the bathroom floor and onto the much more secure footing of the carpet on the landing. As she ran to into her daughter's bedroom, she was relieved to see Stephanie lying in her cot still sound asleep.

The relief soon turned to fear as she realised they were no longer alone in the house. She made her way out of daughter's bedroom and, very slowly, walked down the landing towards the spare room which overlooked the back of the house. It was also the room which that was situated above the fireplace. The room was empty besides a small two-seater sofa and television which sat on a wooden stand that Jane sometimes used when she had friends over. The door was open and the room was empty. No small child, nothing besides the sound of her own heartbeat racing fast. She grabbed her dressing gown which she wrapped around her naked body and lifted her daughter from her bed and left the house. She drove all the way to her mother-in-law's house, in Poultney Road, Woodford. She would sooner be there with Ellen than at home by herself. Or with whatever else was inside her home that afternoon.

Chapter Six. Belief.

Ellen listened to Yvonne explain how the activity had panned out, she watched as her eyes swelled with anticipation and her throat become dry as she spoke about vacant voices and children's footsteps. Without explaining why, Ellen believed every word that Yvonne said. She only had to see the terror hidden deep within her eyes to feel her fear. A glimpse of the paranormal has the same effect on every one of us. The unknown brings unexplained and unanswered questions to the forefront of everyone's thoughts.

When Yvonne was done with the storytelling, Ellen sat still for a moment, not knowing what to say and not wanting to aggravate the situation.

"You believe me don't you, Ellen?" Yvonne asked, taking a long sip of her black coffee, flinching as the boiling drink scorched her upper lip.

"What a silly thing to ask," Ellen said as she leant into Steph's car seat and tickled her belly, "what do *you* think it was?"

Yvonne sat for a moment, she put down her cup into its saucer and looked about the kitchen. She thought about all of the horrors and the stories she had been told about the house on Poultney Road and of her own experiences there too, but as she looked about the large, fairly modern and more than adequate kitchen, she could not help but love it. She knew why Ellen wanted to stay living there, why she had such an attachment to the place, the memories that had grown there and the connection she believed it had to her husband.

"Do you think it was Richard who was haunted, or this house?" The words left her lips quicker than she knew how to stop them.

Neither women spoke. Ellen stood from her chair and walked over to the kitchen sink, looking out of the small window into the garden, "I don't know," she replied, finally. "I thought it was just Richard, I thought that once he died, the ghosts would leave this place and find whatever peace they were looking for, but now I'm not so sure."

"What do you mean, Ellen? Has something happened?"

"More, than I want to share," she replied, lost somewhere between the question and the real answer she could have given.

*****

Flo had stayed in Claybury hospital since her fall six months earlier. It was not an ideal place to send someone you cared so much about. It was a psychiatric hospital full of people who were in a much worse state than Flo, but her doctors said it was the best hospital in the area for a patient with Alzheimer's.

Ellen had made the family aware that Flo's condition was worsening, not that Yvonne left it too long before each visit but Ellen was keen for her to visit sooner rather than later. It was a bright Friday afternoon. Jane was at school, Eric at work and Steph was at Elsie and Mervyn's house so Yvonne dropped into the local florists in Sawbridgeworth and picked up a bouquet of red carnations. As she approached the hospital grounds via a long, narrow path, the first thing that Yvonne saw was the water tower. It stood tall, overlooking the grounds. Yvonne looked up the large red-brick building as she approached it. From a distance it did not look half as grand as it actually was, with large windows scattered across its large frontage. Most of the building was hidden behind towering pine trees that were mostly bare of leaves even though it was mid-summer. The sun was hiding behind pockets of grey clouds,

62

leaving the huge building in its own shadows. *I bet this place has a few ghosts of its own,* Yvonne thought, as she took a sharp right into the visitor's car park. If only she had known about the horrific experiments and tests that were taking place inside, she may have tried to get Flo moved to another hospital. Just as we do now, Yvonne and the rest of the Camp family trusted the doctor's better judgements and did as they advised.

Straightening out her black knee-length skirt and sheer navy, blouse, Yvonne approached the main entrance, subconsciously taking in a deep breath and clearing her mind of hauntings and ghosts. When she approached the reception, the nurse checked Flo's details and sent Yvonne in a different direction than she had been in the times when she had visited before. "We had some problems with Flo yesterday," she told her, "she wouldn't eat or drink. She was becoming a little irrational, saying something about a woman not wanting to leave her side. So we put her in the quiet ward, they keep a better watch of patients there. If you follow the signs to the water tower, you will come to her ward, it would be hard to miss"

The nurse smiled as she waved Yvonne on her way. She hated Claybury, the sounds the patients made; screaming and wailing coming from almost every orifice of the place, were enough to give anyone nightmares. She followed signs to the water tower and only stopped when she came to a doorway at the end of the long, fairly well lit corridor. She stopped because unlike other doors in the hospital, this one was closed. It had a small window in the top half which enabled Yvonne to see that the lights were either off or very dim on the other side. She pushed into the door as it swung open. The door had blocked off yet another corridor, a much darker one. For some reason the lights were switched off and there were no windows, so it was difficult to see where it lead. She much preferred Flo's usual place within the hospital. She had a nice room that overlooked the grounds. There were bars at the window but she could easily see outside. The walk there was easy too, in another, smaller part of the building, away from the screaming and moaning that she could now hear.

Yvonne took two steps into the corridor; as she did she felt something crunch beneath the heel of her shoe. *Cockroaches!* "Yuck!" she exclaimed, the thought causing her own flesh to crawl.

She began to tip-toe, trying to feel her way between the bugs that she could hear scurrying around her feet.

"Pssssst!" she jumped as the sound came again from someone on the other side of the corridor.

"Who's there?" She asked into the darkness.

It was difficult for Yvonne to see properly as the corridor was so poorly lit as the only light was what squeezed its way through the edges of the doors at either end of the long corridor.

"Oi, you!" She heard someone say, "come 'ere."

Yvonne squinted slightly, trying to see what was in front of her and as she did she made out some small, wooden doors that seemed to have bars at the top of them, perhaps they were small windows but they looked like bars. *It must be the people inside the rooms,* she thought, *I hope this isn't the Quiet Ward.*

She took two steps forwards, almost at the door completely, curious to know who it was that was trying hard to get her attention.

"You're a bit of all right, you are. Fancy a quickie? I'll give you sixpence," came the voice again, followed by a roar of laughter that echoed on the empty walls and down the hallway.

Yvonne kicked off her shoes, bending so quickly to pick them up that she almost kneed herself in the face. She no longer cared about the crunching cockroaches and squashed beetles beneath her feet; she could feel them splatter between her toes. The sound of laughter chased her down the long hallway and out through the other door. As soon as she was through it, so she was reunited with the daylight that she had desperately missed. She rested her hands on her knees and bent over like an athlete who had crossed the finish line.

"Can I help you?" came a soft voice from behind her, "you look lost."

Yvonne turned to see a small woman, dressed in a white doctors' jacket. "Yes, please!" She exclaimed, a little more desperate than she had anticipated, "I'm looking for Florence Camp. I was told she was in the Quiet Ward?"

The little lady smiled, her eyes peering over the top of her thick rimmed glasses. "You've come to the right place," she said, "come with me."

*****

Flo was in a room behind the second door along the never-ending corridor. She was sat at the back, near a window, by herself. She looked frailer than the last time Yvonne had come to see her which was almost a week ago. Her woollen cardigan hung on her tiny frame, accentuating just how small she was.

"Hello, Nan," Yvonne said. She may not have been blood related but she was like the Nan Yvonne never had. The women in her family all seemed to die young which was why she followed the moto—no time like the present.

Flo did not move in her chair. Yvonne did not think that she would stand to greet her but she thought she may at least acknowledge her. But Flo did not even flinch at the sound of her voice.

"I bought you some chocolate," Yvonne said, pulling a small bar of Cadburys Dairy Milk from her handbag. Placing it on a round coffee table that was just below the window, in front of where Flo was sitting. She thought it might bring a smile to the elderly woman's face but she remained unmoved. "How are you feeling today? You look like you've had your hair done, it looks lovely."

Yvonne reached forward to play with Flo's hair which was messed in all directions but as her fingers swept the top of Flo's head, a small, wrinkled hand reached up and grabbed her wrist. "She was here last night, Eve, you know, that woman that Robert saw, in Poultney Road," frustration smothered her face as Yvonne watched, confused. "Oh, you know who I mean, the woman in white, the one who had the long grey hair. They always tried to hide things from Henry and I, thought we didn't know what was going on. But we knew and Robert told us everything about that night. We saw things of our own you know, we had our own hauntings up there that we didn't tell anyone about; things what would make your skin crawl. But last night when that … that woman came to me, I just knew she wasn't finished with us lot yet." Flo continued, leaning forwards in her armchair towards Yvonne who was speechless, she couldn't believe the words that were coming out of the old woman's mouth. Flo gripped tighter onto Yvonne's arm, almost too strong to be the grasp of an elderly woman. "You see, those old ghosts that were in Poultney Road don't haunt the house, they haunt us; Richard bought them back here and they blame us for their torment—for their inability to rest in peace." Flo laughed, just a small chuckle that sent a chill down Yvonne's spine, "but the man in black, you know, the one who followed Richard his whole life? He only used Richard as a portal, a way of connecting to the living, I think its Ellen he wants and now that Richard's dead, she's more susceptible, opened herself up for contact." Flo's eyes never left Yvonne's, "they'll never leave; they have nowhere else to go. There's no point running away," she laughed again but this time, she lowered her voice, "no matter how fast or far you run, they will always follow close behind."

*****

Flo never made it out of the Quiet Ward; in fact she never got to see anyone else before she died which was just three days after Yvonne's visit. They thought it was a heart attack which found her in her sleep. If any method of dying was pleasant then to go peacefully whilst sleeping was probably it, and being ninety-nine years old, just three months away from celebrating with a letter from the Queen, Flo did not do too badly.

The day Yvonne went to visit Flo in the chapel of rest in Woodford, she could not shake the memory of her last visit to Claybury hospital. She knew that the episode was more than likely connected to the Alzheimer's disease, but there was just a small piece of her niggling away at her conscience, compelling her to tell Ellen or Eric of the things Flo had said about the ghosts which had haunted her, but she could not. The family were mourning their loss and she felt she would only add worry to their concerns.

When she reached the chapel, the priest was waiting at the doors, "Reverend Green?" Yvonne asked, shaking the elderly man's hand who looked almost as old and frail as what Flo had been the last time she saw her. "I'm here to see Flo," she said, following him inside.

The air was still warm but the humidity left her at the door. She shivered as she remembered the cardigan she had thrown onto the back seat, *damn*, she thought, stroking her arms vigorously to warm them.

"She's just through those doors there, behind the altar," Reverend Green said, pointing towards the back of the church, "would you like me to come?"

"No, no," Yvonne said quickly, "I'll be fine by myself."

She smiled briefly as she turned her back on the Priest. As she walked down the aisle and right at the altar; all she could think about were the words Flo had said, 'no matter how fast or far you run, they will always follow close

67

behind.' Yvonne's stomach twisted as she remembered. *Are they here now?* She asked herself, *following me to take one last look at Flo, the woman who introduced the Camp's to Poultney Road. The woman who had mothered the man who had bought them back here.* She preferred to think that they had followed her there rather than the idea of them being somewhere else with Flo – not haunting her but trapping her from her own resting place.

She twisted the large, iron knob on the heavy door as she heard the latch drop. The door opened and Yvonne could see Flo laid out in an open coffin. She was the only body in the chapel, which was small and serene; quite picturesque as the sun shone through the glass-stained windows, creating colourful shadows dancing around the room like fairies in a garden. She walked over to the body which was dressed in a tasteful dress and jacket, one she had worn a couple of times before she went into hospital. Yvonne stroked the top of Flo's hair, just as she had tried to do not so long ago whilst she was still alive; this time her hair had been lacquered neatly into the perfect style.

"You would have hated that wouldn't you Flo." Yvonne said, a smile creeping across her face. "Face made up and hair all neat. You rest dear friend, you're with Richard now." Before she could think about it, Yvonne leant forward and kissed Flo's forehead, leaving there a bright red lipstick mark. "Oh my God!" Yvonne cursed, not thinking about where she was. "Oh no! I'm so sorry Flo," she cried as she used the back of her hand to rub at the red stain.

Licking her fingers, she rubbed as much of the lipstick off as she could without taking off the make-up that was already on her face. You see Flo hated make-up, she spent years of her life insulting Yvonne's made up face, used to call her a tart. She meant no harm in it, like a child before they learned their manners; but instead, Flo seemed to have forgotten hers.

The following day was Flo's funeral. There were two
funeral cars. Yvonne, Janet, Ellen, Jane and Claire went in
one and the three boys took the other. Keith had been living
up North for a while with his wife Jean. Work had taken
him there but the death of his Nan had bought him home
and had them both thinking about relocating South.
Amongst other things, the boys got talking about their Nan
and the last time they had seen her. As they pulled into the
church car park, Eric told the story of Yvonne's last visit to
see her in the chapel of rest and had the three of them in
hysterics. The Camps way of dealing with grief was to find
humour in the situation somehow, so instead of crying, they
would always find something to laugh about, and Flo's
funeral had not been any different.

"Look at the boys," Ellen said as she stepped out of the
car, "what are they laughing at?"

Yvonne could only imagine.

*****

Flo was cremated and so the service was fairly quick. Ellen
had invited everyone back to her house on Poultney Road
where she had a full spread, courtesy of Yvonne. Her old
boss and close friend, Barbara was looking after Steph. She
was still too young to understand death and they did not
want to upset her. She was only two years old but she was
pretty observant, spending most of her time running around
and finding peoples possessions (usually important items
like purses and glasses) to either hide or re-deliver. The day
of Flo's funeral was no different. Everyone stayed
downstairs and flitted between the lounge and the kitchen.
Yvonne had put a lot of Steph's toys in the front room
which had a small television and some plush furniture in.
There was nothing in there Steph could harm herself with

and both Claire and Jane were good at keeping an eye on her.

Both girls were sitting in with her. "Shall we grab some food whilst there's still some left?" Jane suggested, standing away from the board game they had been playing for the past hour or so.

They looked at Steph who was transfixed by an episode of *Button Moon* which showed a tall, walking, talking washing up brush getting inside a spaceship made from a baked-bean can and a funnel, "She'll be fine for five minutes," Jane said, "come on."

She grabbed Claire's hand as they exited the room and ran through the crowd in the lounge to get to the buffet, which to their surprise was still well stocked. Steph sat alone in the front room, watching as the spaceship set off into the sky, making its way back to Button Moon as it did at the end of each episode. As the credits rolled, looking about, Steph was suddenly aware that she was alone. She looked back at the television and then over at the closed door, she pushed herself up onto unsteady feet, running across to the door. She tried but her arm was not quite long enough to reach the handle. She dropped onto her bottom as she looked about the room for something else to entertain herself with. There was an armchair with its back to her. It was not a tall back but being as small as she was, Steph could not see over it but was able to just about make out the top of someone's grey, wiry hair.

"Lolly?" She asked but there was no answer, "Lolly?" She asked again as she bent into the downward dog position and pushed her weight onto her feet.

She started trotting towards the chair when the door behind her opened, "Steph!" Claire said, putting down her plate of food and bending down to lift up her cousin. She was only eleven but to Claire, playing with Steph, she was like having a real-life doll to look after. Claire closed the door behind her, "Would you like me to put on another episode?" She asked, making her way across the large, square room.

Claire had not noticed how cold the temperature had become since she left the room just minutes before.

"Lolly," Steph said, pointing across Claire's body in the direction of the blue fabric arm chair in front of them.

Claire stopped in her tracks. She too could see the back of someone's head, a woman's head, covered in sinewy grey hair and yes it did look similar to Lolly Nanny's (so they would call Flo and her love of all things sweet) but as Claire moved closer and around the side of the chair, she could see that as well as being impossible, the person in the chair was not her Nan. A wrist was resting on the arm of the chair. It was thin. So thin that Claire could see the veins bulging through and looked as though the skin was being stabbed by the ulna bone that protruded through it. Her hair was thin and limp but long enough for her to be sitting on it. She was wearing a thin white nightdress which gaped around the arms, showing her modest breasts beneath it.

Claire stepped away, back towards the door.

"Lolly?" Steph asked again, curious of the situation.

"No, not Lolly," Claire said as she turned and ran to the door.

*****

Janet and Robert left shortly after Claire came running into the kitchen, Steph in her arms and tears in her eyes. She told them what had happened and without making too much fuss, they dismissed what their daughter was saying to the relatives and friends who could hear and made their excuses to the rest of the family. Jane had told Yvonne what Claire had told her happened. Steph knew very little of what was going on and that was good. They did not wish to have to tell anyone about who they really thought the woman in white might have been.

71

Chapter Seven. Return of the seventies.

Robert moved out of Poultney Road in 1970 and into a home with his wife, Janet, in Peterborough. After the night of his sixteenth birthday, when he was last visited by the woman dressed in white, he promised himself that he would never re-enter his bedroom inside number 106, and he stayed true to this. His grandparents were pleased with his company throughout the duration of his final years at home and he never had to reacquaint himself with that dark, sinister room. It was not that he thought it was the only place that she would haunt him; it was the familiarity, the smell and the reality of being back inside the room that made everything feel too real for him to bare.

In 1974, Janet gave birth to their daughter, Claire. A beautiful baby whose brilliant blue eyes and smooth, porcelain skin made every woman coo. She settled in well to their modern, three storey townhouse and they made one of the rooms on the second floor into a nursery. Until she was three months old, Claire slept in with Janet and Robert on the third floor but when they moved her into her own room they did not like the thought of her sleeping on a separate floor to them and so took the smaller room next to the nursery whilst Janet was breast-feeding.

On Saturday 26th February 1975, Yvonne got a call from Janet.

"Hi Yvonne, it's me. What are you doing today?" she asked, her voice quiet, somewhat secretive.

"Hi Janet, is everything OK?" Yvonne heard the tremor in Janet's voice. "What's happened?"

"I need you to come over."

Yvonne did not bother dressing her face, she knew something must be wrong for Janet to call so early. She dropped Jane at her parent's house in Epping and got on the M11 motorway as fast as she could, praying that she avoided any traffic. Her nerves were on edge even though she told herself time over that if it was anything serious then Janet would have told her on the phone. *Or would she?* Her eyes darted from her rear-view mirror to her wing mirrors; something in Janet's tone un-eased her.

She pulled her car to a halt and tore off her seatbelt at the same time she tried to climb from her seat, catching her jacket on the buckle.

"Damn it!" she cursed, which was something Yvonne never did; being bought up to believe that women should not use such profanities, she rarely did.

She picked up her pace as she ran across the road that sat in front of her brother and sister-in-law's home, and scuffed her shoe on the gravel as she made her way up the path to their front door. She had checked for Robert's car but it wasn't on the drive so he must be at work. *Everything's fine,* she tried to reassure herself as she knocked so hard on the front door that she almost put her fist through it.

"Yvonne," Janet said with relief as she pulled open the door.

Yvonne made her way inside. The hallway was dark, darker than usual because Janet still had all of the curtains pulled. She ushered Yvonne into the kitchen where it was darker, with the blind pulled down halfway and a bleak, grey outlook. Janet pulled the door to behind her, as Yvonne took a seat.

"I'm so sorry to have called you here like this, I didn't know who else to turn to. Robert is acting like nothing's happened and we don't want to involve Ellen as we know how much stress she's under at the moment," Janet spoke quickly, rushing through her words. "Yvonne, it's found us."

Janet stood silent as Yvonne looked at her, expressionless. "Sorry, you've lost me. What's found you?"

"Whatever it was that haunted Ellen's house, when Robert lived at home and Richard was alive? It's followed us here, to our home."

Yvonne stared into Janet's eyes. She held her palms together as she felt the clammy bond between them. She rubbed them down the front of her black, skinny jeans.

"How do you know?" Yvonne tried to figure out exactly what Janet was saying.

"Last night Robert was late coming home from work; Claire and I couldn't wait any longer for dinner, she was tired and started to fall asleep waiting for him with me downstairs," Janet explained as she joined Yvonne at the table. She pulled back the chair opposite from her, almost sat down but instead, continued to pace. "When he got home, I was annoyed he hadn't let me know or told me in the morning that he was going to be home late as his dinner was in the bin. He apologised and said that he would go check on Claire, get changed and come back down; not to worry about dinner and instead we'd tuck into the chocolate cake I had left over in the fridge."

Yvonne wondered where Janet was going with the story. She was not one for making something out of nothing but as she stood in front of her, hair un-brushed and a make-up free face; she knew that it must be leading somewhere. Eager to get to the point, Yvonne urged.

"Janet, calm down and tell me what's happened."

Janet stopped. She raised her hand and wiped dry her perspiring brow. She took a deep breath and turned to Yvonne, taking the back of the seat she had pulled out earlier and sat herself down onto it.

"It was the woman who visited Robert at Poultney Road; she was here last night, in our home; in our daughter's bedroom, watching her whilst she slept," Janet managed, as her eyes welled with tears. "Robert had left me downstairs, still clearing away after dinner and decided to get changed in the bedroom before making his way in to kiss Claire goodnight. She was sleeping anyway, he didn't see an urgency, but as he was pulling on his pajama bottoms, he heard the creak of Claire's bedroom door, which only does that when you walk in or out—it needs oiling you see."

Yvonne sat silent; taking in Janet's every word.

"Robert said that he could tell something wasn't right straight away and walked out onto the landing. Our room is still next door to Claire's; we've still not gone back upstairs as we don't like leaving her alone on a different floor. He said that he could hear whispering from the room. At first he thought it must be me and I'd come up stairs or that maybe Claire had woken up and was gurgling words to herself, but then he heard me 'clattering about in the kitchen' – or so he put it – but he knew that he wasn't alone up there with her." Janet lowered her head. "If I'd have known, I would have gone straight upstairs, there's no way I would have ignored something like that."

A tear rolled down Janet's cheek, "Don't cry, nothing is your fault. OK?" Yvonne said, as she wiped the tears from her sister-in-laws face, "what happened next?"

"Robert said he listened at the door to see if he was able to hear what, if anything was being said. But as soon as he got close enough, the whispers stopped. He recognised the feeling straight away Yvonne. He said it feels as though someone is watching you from every angle and there's no escape. He pushed the door open, slowly, and there she was; standing over Claire as she slept in bed; her long grey hair, bones protruding through the skin that covered her bare back." Janet sat back in her chair, resting her body, and her thoughts; fixating her gaze onto her fingers that were fiddling with idle pieces of skin that hung around her nail. "It was then that I heard Richards screams; I've never heard him cry like that, he was sobbing, terrified. By the time I reached him on the landing, the woman was gone and he was alone with Claire in his arms." She turned to look at Yvonne, "I don't know how to deal with this. What should we do?"

Yvonne sat for a moment, speechless but then found her words, "Perhaps it was a one off. Perhaps it won't happen again and there's no need to panic," Yvonne suggested as she stroked the smooth skin on Janet's forearm, secretly aware that whatever the woman in white was, had never gone away, she had just been waiting for the right time to return.

"Claire had been at Ellen's yesterday, she was baby-sitting her whilst I went into town to get her birthday presents. When I got back to Poultney Road, Ellen said that she'd been acting odd and was perhaps coming down with something. When I asked what had happened, she was a little vague but said that it was when she took her upstairs to, Claire had reacted badly and started kicking and screaming. Ellen had an awful scratch on her face where Claire's nails had caught her whilst she was having the tantrum. She seemed poorly for a little while after I got her home which is why I wanted to get her to bed early. Do you think, this woman, followed us home?" Janet asked, tears now streaming down her skin onto the pine table that she rested on.

"Where's Robert?" Yvonne asked, distracting Janet momentarily, "why isn't he here with you? Is he OK with everything that's happened?"

"He's taken Claire out for the morning. He was in such a bad state last night but I think he's accepted it now."

"Accepted what?" Yvonne asked.

Janet caught Yvonne's gaze, "that the ghosts from Poultney Road are everywhere."

Chapter eight. A life taken too soon.

The months that followed Flo's funeral, showed little, if no paranormal activity. The supernatural phenomena that Yvonne had been experiencing seemed to be settling also, for a while. It still lingered in the back of her mind, eating away at the endorphins in her body, waking her up at night and plaguing her thoughts.

As with every year that we grow older, the seasons seem to diminish as summer becomes autumn, and winter becomes spring. Before long, in 1985, the days became shorter and the weather, cooler. To prevent the onslaught of winter-fatigue, Eric surprised his family with a trip to Florida. It was not the first time they had visited; owning a business in California meant that the Camps were well acquainted with the country.

*****

They arrived home, two weeks later, jetlagged and drained. A fortnight spent rushing around amusement parks and eating copious amounts of burgers and red meat, always has an adverse effect on people's lifestyles, but conveniently, never until they arrived home. Although desperate to see her parents, show them photos and tell them about their trip, Yvonne called her Mum early Saturday morning and explained that she would give their weekly shopping trip a miss that week as she had too much to do around the house.

"That's OK love, I understand," Elsie said, twiddling the wire of the receiver between her fingers. She had been looking forward to seeing her daughter and the girls but already had it in mind that Yvonne may want to reschedule.

"Mervyn said he'll pop into town with me to pick up dinner for tonight and tomorrow so no need for you to feel bad. You take it easy today and catch up on what needs to be done." Elsie reassured, "and if you find a spare moment tomorrow, perhaps you could pop over with the girls then?"

"Yes, good idea Mum. I'll give you a call later to confirm."

After a moment or two wishing their farewells, Yvonne hung up the phone. She had a million things to do, *where to start?* She asked herself as she dragged the first load of dirty clothes from the suitcase.

*****

It was around four o'clock when the phone rang. The girls were both upstairs in Jane's room, Eric had gone to work to check on the fax machine, as if he needed an excuse. The buzz of the phone startled Yvonne, who was busy, down on her knees, cleaning the kitchen floor; water everywhere and hands to elbow in foam. *Damn it!* She cursed.

"Hello?" she said sternly into the receiver.

There was silence on the other end, "Hello?" she asked again, this time a little more impatiently.

"Yvonne," spoke a low voice on the other end, "it's Dad. There's been an accident."

It did not take Yvonne long to note down the whereabouts of her parents. She called upstairs to Jane, who was playing with Steph and told her to look after her until her father got home from work. She slammed the front door closed behind her, dashed to the car and turned the key in the ignition as fast as possible. She was at Epping hospital within fifteen minutes. She darted through the front doors, past the receptionist and into the emergency unit where Mervyn was sat waiting.

"Dad!" she proclaimed and threw her arms around his neck, holding him there for a moment. "What happened? Where is she?"

Mervyn sat Yvonne down before explaining anything. They had been out shopping in Epping, not for long but long enough for Mervyns' legs to begin to ache and his body became tired. He was in the early stages of Parkinson's disease which for a long time was misdiagnosed, mistreated and misunderstood by most doctors. One thing it did cause was tiredness, and so Elsie sent him to collect the last few bits from the convenience store whilst she nipped into their favourite butcher to pick up their meat for the week.

"It was when I came outside, I was going to walk over to meet Elsie; I would never expect her to carry the bags, especially nothing as heavy as the meat," Mervyn explained, "that was when I saw the crowd of people bustling around her, causing a scene." His eyes were heavy and darker than they usually were, the dampness around them like fresh puddles.

"I just knew, I didn't need to push my way forward, I just knew that the crowds of kids and stall-holders were shielding me from Elsie," he dabbed his eye. "Your Mum's been hit by a car, Yvonne, it was driving too fast and the driver claims that he didn't see her. She's slipped into a coma and they don't know when she's going to wake up."

Mervyn raised his eyes to meet his daughter's. "We might lose her, Eve," the tears began to fall as he collapsed his head into Yvonne's arms that were open and ready to catch him.

Yvonne called her brother, Ben, who met her at the hospital. She called Eric and explained the situation and told him to stay at home with the girls, there were enough people at the hospital, surrounding Elsie's bedside.

"I'll try to come home tonight, I promise," she said as she hung up the phone.

Nothing seemed real; her brain would not comprehend the situation. She sat down, alone by the telephone and thought about the conversation she had with her Mum that morning. Although entirely unbeknown and completely unavoidable, she could not help but blame herself for not visiting that day. Every *what if* passed through her train of thought.

The days that passed were a blur. Yvonne would wake up, dress Stephanie, drop Jane at school, pick up Mervyn and spend the day at the hospital by Elsie's bedside, praying that she would start responding to the sound of their voices, Stephanie's laughter or the medication that they were feeding her. But each day she laid as still as a doll, her face grazed and body bruised from the force of the car that hit her tiny frame. *Bastard,* Yvonne thought as the image forced its way into her.

It was eight days after the accident, a Sunday that Ben came to visit for the fourth time. He found it hard to get the time off from work, and visited as often as time would allow. Jane was at home looking after her sister, whilst Yvonne, Eric, Mervyn and Ben sat around Elsie's bed talking. The chat had dithered from the fundamentals of the accident, to the children and day-to-day chores, anything not to have to discuss or think about the possibility that Elsie might never wake up. Yvonne had to be careful given Mervyn's condition, although the doctors were not as clued up on Parkinson's disease as they should have been, they knew that stress and upset could progress the disease rapidly. Mervyn liked to talk about Jane and Steph, he loved to hear about how well Jane was doing at school, and learn about the silly things that Stephanie had said or done.

"I'm going to nip outside for a cigarette, I won't be a minute," Ben assured as he kissed his sister on the forehead, "come and get me if anything happens." Something he said and would later come to regret it.

Ben had only been gone a couple of minutes when it happened. In the grand scheme of things it was such a small atom in the universe and yet it had such a huge and lasting impact.

Elsie moved.

Yvonne was sitting on her left side, Mervyn on her right. They had gotten used to talking to her subconscious, hoping that somewhere deep inside her sleep, she could hear them. It was whilst they were talking quietly between themselves, that they heard it. It was like a rattle deep in her throat, like she was clasping onto life. It caused both Yvonne and Mervyn to stop talking, and switch their attention back onto their wife and mother who was laying helpless on the bed in front of them.

"Elsie, sweetheart," Mervyn said as he rose to his feet, squeezing hold of his wife's hand.

Yvonne called for a nurse, "Come quick! Nurse, nurse! I think my Mum's waking up."

As Yvonne returned to her mother's bedside, holding on tight to her limp hand, she watched Elsie turn her head only slightly before release. The noise stopped. The only sound breaking the awful silence was the clatter of trolleys being pushed by nurses in the next room.

The nurse who responded to Yvonne's cries for help, lowered her head, "I'm so sorry, what you just heard was the 'death rattle'; a sound that the body makes as it lets go of life."

Yvonne looked up at the nurse, "What are you saying?"

"I'm so sorry, but Elsie has passed away."

Chapter Nine. No fair sentence.

Yvonne left it until after the court case to suggest sorting through Elsie's belongings. The man who had knocked Elsie down and caused her to have a fatal stroke, was charged with dangerous driving, fined and given no further conviction. The fact that he had to live with taking another persons' life and the nightmares that would hopefully haunt him, were the only real punishment that Yvonne believed he had.

It was two weeks later that Yvonne went over to her father's bungalow with her daughters to start the process. As they walked up the long, enchanted path that lead to the front door, Yvonne noticed that her father had not been tending to the flower beds in the way he usually would and even their prize-winning roses were withering.

"Dad," Yvonne took her father's face in her hands, she felt the rough of his stubble on the surface. "Steph's been looking forward to seeing you all morning."

Mervyn leant down to kiss his youngest granddaughter's tiny forehead which felt warm against his lips. Her spindly little arms wrapped around his calves, "Granddad!" she exclaimed, as Jane too, greeted Mervyn with an open-arm embrace.

Yvonne stood back and watched through blurred vision as her family comforted each other's grief through a shared moment of compassion. Her family, like everyone else's, was getting smaller by the day. It was all part of life's plan, she knew that, but it didn't make it any easier. Her heart throbbed watching the love that grew in her father's eyes and the smiles that smothered her daughter's faces as they snuggled into their grandfather's chest. She quickly wiped the tears from her eyes before they had time to mark her makeup, she didn't want her girls to see her upset. She didn't want to share that moment with anyone, it was private and she wanted to keep it for herself; locked away somewhere in her memory that she could return to in years to come.

They all made their way inside the house, one behind the other, sheltering themselves from the rain. The weather outside was dismal. As usual, the forecasters had predicted light showers but instead they got a continual downpour that had so far lasted twelve hours without stop. It was hammering it down so hard it sounded like the heavens had opened and unleashed pellets made to destroy the earth; the sound was an echo that repeated so furiously that it could have been mistaken for one continuous roar. It reminded Yvonne of when she and Eric had taken Jane away in their caravan to Newquay when she was not much older than eight. The usually beautiful countryside had been beaten by howling winds and rain so hard it kept them awake all night, every night. This time the rain seemed to mirror the occasion, an oppressive weight on the heart, making the job of sorting through a loved-ones' memories even more difficult to bear.

Mervyn was still in tethers. His shake had developed somewhat over the past few weeks and had spread to his lower limbs. He had visited the doctor the month before with Yvonne, who had encouraged him to be honest about the progression of his disease since his wife passed two months previous. They had suggested increasing the dosage of his medication, Sinemet, with the promise that it might lighten the shake and encourage better movement of his limbs. At the time he was also taking a concoction of pills for his angina and high blood pressure. He had a five-valve bypass a few years previous so it was important, all round, to keep his anxiety at a minimum.

The problem with taking a cocktail of pills were the side effects. The doctor had warned that the combination of Warfarin, Sinemet and other drugs could play havoc with his mind and could cause him to suffer severe hallucinations. It was not long after he increased his Parkinson drug that he introduced Stephanie to some magical fairy creatures in the garden (she, of course, loved the idea and his rather colourful visions encouraged her over-zealous imagination). He'd called Yvonne the week before, in the early hours of the morning, utterly distressed that he had managed to catch a giant rat in the garage and told her to come quick. When she arrived still dressed in her bed-clothes and slippers covered only by her long silk dressing gown, she found instead a small black cushion that Elsie had used for her stitch-work caught beneath the rugged towel that laid sprawled across the stone garage floor. Looking back, Yvonne found herself smiling. She tried to find humour in such moments, because otherwise they might become too difficult to bear.

To make the ordeal less stressful for Mervyn, Jane had agreed to help the following weekend by sorting through all of Elsie's belongings and also their shared items. Yvonne was working long hours, caring for her father, two daughters and working part-time at the school. She barely had time to sleep and with her father needing more and more care, she was losing the time to share between them. She had mentioned to Mervyn a couple of times about looking at possible homes where he may like to stay. He was not short of a penny or two and had ample savings to pay for the very best care. Yvonne believed at the start that she would be able to look after him and had considered moving to a house with an annex, or had enough land to build one, where he could stay close by, but she knew that what he needed was twenty-four hour care; especially as his Parkinson's disease progressed. He agreed to let them have a clear out with the intention of getting a nurse or more regular place to stay where he would be looked after properly.

They spent hours looking through wardrobes, and Jane had fun trying on Elsie's outfits, modeling them and allowing both Mervyn and Yvonne to reminisce on the memories.

They had several bags: a charity shop bag; a rubbish bag; Yvonne's sentimental bag; Jane's fancy-dress bag, and a bag of memories that Mervyn wanted to keep. Yvonne already had the jacket that her mother was wearing the day of the accident, bolero-styled that was adorned with tan coloured, faux fur that had the odd scattering of her mother's blood. No doubt, certain members of the family would find such things morbid or inappropriate for her to keep a piece of clothing that had a memory so tragic attached to it but Yvonne considered it to be the closest thing of her Mum's that she could keep. The last thing that she wore, that carried the sweet smell of her perfume, traced the fibres of her skin and carried strands of her hair. It was a comforting garment she would keep forever, with no intention of ever ridding her cupboard of.

At six o' clock and almost complete with their mission, Yvonne decided to call it a night.

"It's getting late Dad, Eric will be home and wondering where his dinner is," she smiled as she stroked down a tuft of Steph's hair that was sticking up on the top of her head. "Are you sure you don't want to come back for a while, Dad, I know you've eaten but you could watch TV with Eric, I hate the thought of you being here alone," she said as she looked into his watchful eyes.

"I'll be fine, dear. You get yourself home. I'll watch some daft game-show no doubt and then make my way to bed. I'll see you tomorrow and I'll be looking forward to it."

The next day was Monday and he was right, Yvonne would be round the next day with Stephanie to finish the tidying up. Yvonne felt her limbs drag and eye lids were getting heavier by the minute, exhausted from the day's work, both physically and mentally. "As long as you're sure, Dad. I'll see you tomorrow, I promise."

The four of them said their goodbyes and after just five minutes into the journey, both Jane and Steph were sound asleep with Yvonne wishing she could join them.

*****

That night Yvonne dreamt of her childhood, about the years she had shared with her brother growing up. Hearing her father's tales of the war he had returned home from when she was still a small child. About the strength and courage he and the other soldiers had to fight in such a devastating battle. The images floating in front of her eyes showed her scenes of his escape, when he had been captured by the Germans in Italy and taken to a Nazi camp where he was starved and beaten. The dark visions repeated through her retinas, underneath eyelids that were flickering from the images. The mud he had dug his way through, the darkness that filled the tunnel he built; the lack of air, the confined space that was met by a beaming light at the end of the tunnel. The beautiful scene that he'd described and had hung in their family home - a painting by an artist who replicated the scene of soldiers and encouraged their recollections of freedom. She watched the moment from her father's eyes, the darkness that was replaced by a brilliant light. The glistening lake that was below him like an emerald in the hands of a thief. She watched as the stream flowed with the wind, moving fast and carrying away the fear that had built up inside. Then she saw her. A lost child in search of her parents.

"Yvonne? Yvonne?" she heard her mother call, but she was not able to shout back, as much as she tried, she was mute and was slowly losing the ability to breathe.

"Go back, don't leave, go back!" Elsie called, although her expression was distressed, her youthful beauty had returned.

Elsie began pacing up and down the waters-edge, tugging at her hair, clearly stressed and needing help. *What is she doing?* Yvonne questioned within her dream, *what is she telling me?* She watched as the image of her mother remained in front of her as she continued to behave irrationally. She looked up at Yvonne, her warm eyes locked against hers as she smiled and sat herself down by the side of the lake. The flow of the water stopped and everything in the serene landscape stood still besides Elsie. Yvonne, watched as her mother took off her shoes and her stockings and rolled the left with the right. She looked back up at her daughter and said, "Never lose sight of what's in front of you. Never dismiss curiosity," and with those words, she was gone.

Yvonne sat bolt upright, breathing fast as small pebbles of perspiration formed on her forehead like raindrops on glass. She looked down at her sleeping husband and sighed aloud, the tears welling in her eyes. What she would not give to see her mother, to hear her voice. She rested her head back down on her pillow as she fell asleep asking herself over and over again what she should be looking for.

*****

The next day, Yvonne returned to Mervyn's house, Steph in tow and today dressed like a pirate. Her tomboyish ways shone threw her outfit choices; getting her to wear a dress was wasted effort so she let her daughter wear what she loved. Yvonne thought that perhaps the eye patch and pirates hat may give her Dad something to smile about, for a while at least.

He was pleased to see her, the weather had improved over night and the sun was shining. The bungalow was a much lighter, happier place to be and this transferred to their spirits. They had almost finished sorting through Elsie's clothes; through the cupboards and the drawers and

90

all of the places that would usually be a woman's private domain, but which death altered and made anyone's business. They finished off sorting through her underwear and hosiery drawer, most of the contents they intended on discarding and had the black bin bag labelled *RUBBISH* at the ready.

"I had a dream last night, Yvonne; your mother visited me." Yvonne stopped what she was doing for the moment and looked up at her father who was sitting down on the edge of the bed, gazing out of the window. "She looked beautiful, so peaceful. Do you think it might really have been her, telling me that she's OK now?" He looked at his daughter with hope in his eyes, "do you think that's possible?"

Yvonne did not answer as she recalled her own dream she had the night before. Yes, she did think it was possible, she thought that was exactly what had happened. For some reason her mother had chosen to show herself through a dream to both her and her father. There must have been a reason, it couldn't have been a coincidence.

"Dad, this is important, you must try to remember—did Mum say anything? In your dream, did she tell you or ask you anything?"

"No love, I don't think she did. She just smiled at me and before I could touch her, before I could reach out or say anything, I'd woken up and she was gone. Why, what's the matter?"

Yvonne turned to look at Stephanie who was sitting in the middle of the clutter, with her pirate's eye patch and ripped trousers. Whilst she was watching her daughter, she noticed that the pair of stockings she was holding in her hands, that she'd pulled out of the black bin bag marked *RUBBISH* looked oddly swollen, padded with something on the inside. Yvonne crawled forward on her hands and knees and reached forward to take the stockings from Steph who giggled as her mother tickled her tummy to entice her into letting go. Yvonne felt the stockings were thicker, heavier than what they should be. She pulled one from the other and sure enough, inside there was hiding a wad of cash, notes, folded and rolled into one another.

"Oh my God, Yvonne, is that money?" Mervyn asked as he saw his daughter pull the stash from its hiding place.

She looked up her father and smiled, "There's at least five hundred pounds here and there's more where that came from. I know it."

All in all they found between them more than fifteen-hundred pounds of hard earned money her mother had been saving for Mervyn's seventieth birthday. That's what the dream was about, she was telling Yvonne not to throw everything out, to look for what was in front of her. The dream was also her way of saying goodbye, perhaps she wasn't able to rest in peace until she had passed on the money that she had worked so hard for. It was obvious that she had been saving for Mervyn's seventieth birthday; she would have no need to save that sort of money otherwise. Yvonne remembered her mentioning something about a party a few months before her death. Elsie never showed herself in dreams again, she never appeared to Yvonne and only ever to Mervyn when the drugs took hold of his brain and controlled his actions. Father and daughter shared something special that day and they thanked Elsie for her last act of kindness.

Chapter ten. Pocket full of posies.

When any family member dies, it's going to be painful; a pain like no other that does not subside with a hug. And no matter how many pills you pop, the sick feeling does not leave your stomach; not for a long time. An echo that repeats throughout your system, returning when you least expect it. For Yvonne, losing her mother was not just about loss, heartbreak or grief, it was also about the health and anxiety of her father who did not know life without Elsie. She worried about how he would adapt to living life alone.

The money had been a huge surprise, but it was not as though he needed it. Even though Elsie was not around to throw a party for Mervyn, it encouraged Yvonne to pull herself together for her father's sake and arrange the party for him that her mother wanted him to have. Yvonne rarely put herself first; it was a trait she had developed from a young age. She would always take the blame for things she never did, owned up to almost everything and stood up for what she believed in. It was in her nature. She was kind-hearted, unfortunately a characteristic you do not often find in people. From the moment she had lost her mother, she knew that no matter how sick her father got, she would look after him the best she could and in a way that her mother would have been proud of. Although she had two children, Jane was at an age that she spent most of her time at school or wanted to be around her friends, and Steph was young enough to be happy to follow her mother everywhere, and this she did. It became a regular thing that after dropping Jane at school, or at the train station, Yvonne stopped at the local supermarket to pick up some bits for Mervyn before heading over to his house.

On July 13, 1986, Yvonne had stuck with her usual, daily routine, had dropped Jane at school and picked up some fresh fish, potatoes and vegetables for her father to

have that evening. The fish would be lunch. Mervyn
cooked the very best fish suppers; the smell of fresh
haddock would fill the kitchen, along with the mouth-
watering aroma of home-baked chips. It was the one meal
he excelled in and had always been Elsie's favourite too
when she had been alive. Stephanie would always settle
herself on one of the tall, leather bar stools in the kitchen,
hands resting on the wooden work-surface that mounted the
high-end fashion cream cupboards with brown, wood-effect
trim. Steph had learnt that when she visited her
grandparents' house, if she was good and ate all of her
dinner, she would usually be rewarded with an ice-pop of
her choice. It had always been Elsie's job to supply the ice
pops but since she had passed, Steph would always manage
to sweet-talk Mervyn and get a blue-raspberry flavour
every time. She did not know that this meant he had ended
up with boxes full of three other flavours in the freezer but
she probably would not have cared anyway. Mervyn did
not mind, he just loved to see how her mouth and lips
turned blue without her realising.

"It's a glorious day, Dad, shall we go to the cemetary
after lunch?" Yvonne asked, pulling a small, sharp, bone
from her tooth. "We can pick up some nice flowers from
town on the way."

Mervyn nodded, he liked her suggestion.

"Everything OK, Dad?" Yvonne asked, concerned about
her father's silence.

He had become quieter since his wife had died. Whether
it was the Parkinson's disease, the drugs or the grief,
Yvonne wasn't sure, but she did like to check in from time
to time that it wasn't anything else.

"Everything's fine sweetheart," he replied as he pushed
his fish around the plate.

His appetite had suppressed but that was only to be
expected, given the circumstances. Once he had finished
eating all that he could stomach, Mervyn walked around the

94

island Steph was sat at and reached into the freezer; the cold frost momentarily stunning him. He grabbed the single blue pop that was lying dormant alongside its half-full box and used a pair of kitchen scissors to snip off the end. Trimming back the sharp edges and wrapping in kitchen towel, he handed the ice lolly to Steph, who was eagerly awaiting her treat.

"Thanks, Granddad!" she exclaimed, unable to hide the excitement; he could not help but grin at the sound of her finally pronouncing Granddad properly.

Yvonne tidied around, cleaned off the plates and fetched her father's jacket. Three times a week they visited Elsie's grave in Pardon Wood Cemetery, not far from where Mervyn lived. Unlike many cemeteries, Pardon Wood was a truly beautiful place to be. It was peaceful, surrounded by countryside and freshly cut grass, often they would find widows and children picnicking at their loved-ones graves. Stephanie was often lucky enough to catch the ice cream man who visited occasionally.

Today was a great day for her, her cheeks and lips already smothered in a sticky blue film from the ice pop she had devoured an hour or so before, Stephanie tugged on the sleeve of her mother's thin, cream cardigan,

"Mummy, mummy!" she cried, "please can I have an ice cream?" she begged, emphasising the vowels in the word 'please'.

"Here you go," Mervyn said as he handed her a shiny new pound coin, "spend it wisely," he winked at Yvonne as he followed Steph over to the van parked up on the small pebble road which ran through the grounds not far from Elsie's grave.

Yvonne did not mind her father spoiling her daughter. Steph's frame was tiny, she was extremely active, never sat still for longer than a minute so she was not ever concerned about the sugar she consumed, it probably kept her going. As she turned to watch her father and daughter run to the

95

ice cream van, she noticed a woman tending to a grave two down from where Elsie was resting. The grave looked newly polished, a grand white stone which stood tall. Yvonne's eyes were good and she was able to see a small photograph in the top centre of the grave. It was of a young boy, maybe seventeen. He was handsome and too young to be buried. In front of his grave were at least fifteen small cone-shaped vases sticking out from the ground full of carnations – some white, some red – they were fresh, no older than a day or two. Beautiful. In front of the grave stood a woman who looked a similar age to Yvonne, her eyes were red and swollen, her skin was blotchy. She looked like she had been crying for days. Yvonne looked away before the woman could catch her eye. She knew that the grave could not have been there long as each row was formed in order; he must have died recently, in the last few weeks.

Yvonne felt her eyes well with tears, not only because of the grief she was feeling for the loss of her dear mother, but for the pity she felt for the poor woman standing beside her. *To lose a child,* she thought, *every parent's most devastating nightmare.*

Before the tears had time to fall, Stephanie was back by her side. She threw herself down in a cross-legged position on the grass. "Look Mummy, I got a 99 Flake!" she said as she shoved the ice cream into her tiny mouth. "Yummmmm!"

"Stephanie, eat with your mouth closed," Yvonne laughed as the ice cream covered the blue stain her daughter already had coated around her mouth.

For a while, she and her father pulled back the weeds and laid down fresh flowers. Steph helped by patting down the grass that sprung up around the grave.

After around five minutes, Steph had lost all interest in the grave and had stood watching, as if transfixed at something on the far-side of the cemetery.

"Mummy, can I go play with those children?" Steph asked, "They're singing my favourite nursery rhyme," she said, as she skipped off towards the back of the cemetery.

"Dad, go follow her please," Yvonne said as she lifted herself from kneeling position to look over where her daughter was running too.

Mervyn left immediately but the Parkinson's disease caused him to shuffle his feet slowing down his pace. Yvonne watched for a moment but retired to her gardening.

"Excuse me," a small voice interrupted her, "I hope you don't mind me introducing myself? My name's Beverley." Yvonne looked up, having to squint her eyes as the sun shone directly into her gaze. It was the woman who had previously caught Yvonne's attention, tending two graves along.

Leaving her small shovel on the ground, "Hi Beverley, I'm Yvonne, it's nice to meet you."

"Sorry if this seems a little strange, it almost definitely will—watching your daughter has made my blood run cold," Beverley lifted her arm and pointed over to where Stephanie was now playing, "look over at your daughter."

Yvonne turned from Beverley and looked over at Steph. She was standing, with both of her arms stretched out to the sides, fists clenched. She appeared to be skipping in a circle; a circle of nothing—no one else was there. She could see that her daughter was laughing, giggling; she looked like she was singing.

Yvonne turned back to face Beverley, "where your daughter is playing, that's where the children are laid to rest. There are more than a hundred children buried in that part."

Yvonne looked back at where Stephanie was playing and had bumped herself to the ground, laughing harder than she had before. Her eyes were playful and her actions were as though they were being encouraged by someone or something else playing with her. Yvonne's knees trembled

97

and her legs felt like they had been shot with an anesthetic. She found it in her to run as fast as her legs could carry her, to her daughter, over-taking Mervyn who had just reached Stephanie himself. She whisked her daughter up into her arms, "It's time to go," she spoke softly in her father's ear.

"Mummy! Why did you do that for?" Stephanie cried, "You frightened all of the children away!"

*****

Yvonne did not want to worry Mervyn, he no doubt, thought she was a little strange behaving the way she did at the cemetery, but she hoped he had put it down to grief. She dropped him home and being the nice day that it was, let Jane walk home from the train station with her friends.

In fact, she did not tell anyone about what happened that day; she decided to keep it to herself. She did not question Steph, she didn't want to make a big thing of it but she was worried that if anything else happened, she may have to.

Chapter eleven. The perfect place.

It was not long before Yvonne made the very tough decision that Mervyn should be cared for in a residential home. The combination of Parkinson's disease and the concoction of pills he was popping meant that he was not in a stable frame of mind and needed twenty-four hour care. The hallucinations had gotten worse and in September of 1986 he had thought that someone was trying to break into his house. It was not until the police were called out to his home that it was explained to him that the noises he honestly believed to be someone kicking down the door, were in fact no more than the storm that was causing a lot of commotion outside.

If she could have offered him the care he needed, or if their house had been large enough to offer her father a room there, Yvonne would not have ever let him go into a home, but it was what was best for him and they both knew it.

The search for a respectable home took no longer than a few weeks. Yvonne had heard a few stories associated with elderly people's homes. About the patients being left unattended and not given the correct level of attention and care that they were, in fact, paying for. They had looked at several local homes but none of them were at the standard that Yvonne wanted for her father. They either did not have the grounds for him to enjoy walks, a library for him to read or the rooms were not adequate enough. Mervyn may have Parkinson's disease and needed the odd hand every now and again, but he was not bed ridden and so the surroundings and location were important to the decision making process.

Yvonne stumbled upon Weasendale House by pure chance. You often hear all the horror stories of places and people's experiences and it would seem the little gems always fell under the radar. Bad news travels fast; good news doesn't.

It was one day when Yvonne took Mervyn to see a home near Woodford that they saw a sign for Weasendale House.

"What's Weasendale?" Yvonne asked as she slowed down at the red light. There was a small, yellow sign with an arrow pointing right attached to the traffic lights.

Mervyn did not reply, he just sat looking in the direction that the sign was pointing.

"Let's go take a look." Yvonne suggested as she pulled away.

She had no idea that Weasendale House was an elderly people's home but curiosity ran its course. Steph was in the back of the car, playing with her *Glo Worm* that she took everywhere with her. It was frayed around the edges and the colours were fading but she loved squeezing and watching it light up; it was something that never seemed to bore her and on this particular day, had conveniently kept her amused.

As Yvonne turned the corner, the road was crowded with trees, like people queuing in line; they stood tall, hovering over the narrow, winding road. Even though the sun was still fairly high in the sky, the shadows from the tree absorbed any light shining down and the road felt forgotten. No traffic, no people, just trees dividing the road from the forest on both sides. Mervyn spotted a small sign on the left side of the road:

WEASENDALE HOUSE

And an arrow pointing them to turn right down an even smaller, darker and more twisting road. Yvonne looked round at her father, who was already looking at her. It was as though they were driving straight onto the set of a horror movie, until, that is, they reached the opening of a driveway, unveiling a beautiful, bright building with floor-to-ceiling windows covering an enclosed porch and a

100

quaint, little wooden front door with a welcome plaque above it.

"Well, this looks a little more promising," Yvonne said as they pulled onto the gravel drive, bringing her car to a halt.

She caught her father looking up at the red-brick building with a glint in his eye and a smile creasing his lip, "I like this one sweetheart," he said, as he took his daughter's hand and kissed it.

Neither one of them needed much persuading from the current owner, Ms Kilston although she insisted upon being called Kimberley—the place sold itself. It came with a higher price tag but the sale of Sanddown—the five bedroom home Mervyn and Elsie shared together—along with the sale of the bungalow, meant Mervyn could enjoy many years at Weasendale House.

Kimberley introduced them to the nurses, who were all keen to make them both feel at home. They all fell in love with Steph who was offering out handfuls of jellies that she had stashed in her pocket. She had been taught never to accept sweets from strangers but she had never been told that there was any harm in handing them out to them.

The three of them were guided around the building, the long corridors and inside the rooms which were all a nice size and comprised a bed, wardrobe, chest of drawers and even a small television. They had views of the gardens at the back of the house and it was this that had them signing on the dotted line. They did not need to go away and discuss anything, they both knew this was the place Mervyn would see out his days and when he walked out the back patio doors and into the beautiful gardens, he did not need any more persuading. The luscious green lawn was surrounded by an enclosed forest of trees and wildlife. Stephanie even pointed out several rabbits that were roaming the grounds.

"I'm sure you're going to be very happy here, Mervyn. There are other people here with Parkinson's disease so we all know a lot about your condition and you will have a lot of friends," Kimberley said as she walked the family out to their car.

Mervyn smiled at his daughter, the kind of smile that did not need words. It was enough for Yvonne to see the relief on her father's face and to know that he would be happy again living somewhere other than his own home.

*****

Mervyn settled into Weasendale House quickly and it was only four weeks later that a carers position came up. It was not obvious whether Kimberly had created the vacancy with Yvonne in mind but she jumped at the opportunity. With no nurse or carer training, Yvonne was simply a spare pair of hands, to help the elderly when they needed her. She organised games like Bingo and charades which everyone loved. She bought the most thoughtful gifts and spent any money she earned on the prizes. But it was not about the money, it never was; it was about being there for her father whenever he needed her most. It gave her the opportunity to do what she had wanted to do right from the start—to look after him.

Stephanie was only five but she loved spending time with all of the elderly people. They took her for walks in the grounds—or rather, she took them on walks. She would knock on all of the doors and offer round sweets. She loved helping her mother when they played games and often ran round all of the tables, marking off the bingo cards when the numbers were called out as many of the residents would have fallen asleep before the game came to an end.

Stephanie got along with all of the residents at Weasendale but one resident in particular. Her name was Mary.

Chapter Twelve. Curiosity killed the cat.

You could tell she was once beautiful. The glisten in her emerald green eyes captivated a thousand memories. In her teens, no doubt, she broke a thousand hearts. Her hair, once as dark and luscious as an Andalusian horse's mane and her pale, crinkled skin would have once been youthful with any imperfection ironed out. Until January 1987, she had always kept to herself, not once getting involved in group activities and opting to dine alone each evening. She was a loner, hiding in the shadow of the woman she once was.

Her late husband, Ivan, had lost his battle with cancer ten years ago and she had been a recluse since; never wanting to risk getting close to anyone. Never wanting to experience the pain of losing someone again.

She had been a resident at Weasendale House for three years. Her family were too busy to find time for her and although she did not really need a carer, putting her in a home took her from their hair. She was staying in room number nine, next door to Mervyn, who had been assigned room ten after taking a liking to it during his tour. Initially Mervyn was uninterested in making friends, he minded his own business and got on with his own routine, but when he noticed Mary sitting alone every night and retiring to her room hours before the others; he felt obliged to introduce himself.

Even though he too was older now, his mechanics slower and skin ever-so-slightly looser; Mervyn's Mediterranean good-looks and kind manner always caught the attention of women. Mary, however, saw deeper than his exterior, she felt his warm, loving heart and generous way and it was inevitable they would soon become close friends.

Of course, befriending Mervyn, also meant that Mary became acquainted with Steph. As far as little girls went,

Steph had an odd attraction to older people. She had the ability to get them talking and make them laugh, even when their hearing may have been slightly impaired or their sight failing, she would be happy walking through the gardens with them and helping pick their prizes from their wins at bingo. She was the perfect assistant for Yvonne and Mary loved her. Often Steph would wander into Mary's room and take both her and Mervyn down to the bright conservatory at the front of the house where she would sit for hours and let Mary talk about old stories of her children and Steph would recite dance routines she had learnt at school.

As Yvonne spent more time at Weasendale House than she did at home, Steph spent a lot of time running the halls and roaming the grounds. Fantasy and make believe became second nature to her and the large manner house was a blank canvas for her wild stories and adventures. As time passed, the more lenient Yvonne became with letting Steph spend time in the home alone; accompanying the patients and playing in the halls. The only place Steph was not allowed to roam was the basement. The door was more than often locked as it was an old, unused space under the grounds.

On 8th July 1989, Yvonne and Steph dropped Jane off at her friend's house and on their way to the home, they stopped at the Village Tearooms in Epping for a full-English. Steph's eyes were always way too big for her miniscule stomach but Yvonne loved to watch her eyes light up as the waitress walked over with her man-sized meal.

They finished up their food and Yvonne paid the bill. They got to Weasendale before Yvonne was due. She never followed her shifts and worked extra hours because being there with her father was not a job, it was a pleasure.

The weather outside was warm, humid in fact, and Steph whipped her cardigan off as soon as she made it inside. She had taken a ball with her and some other normal toys you might expect of a six year old child, but she also took with her a notebook, pen and some lens-free glasses she had found hiding under the sofa in the sitting room at home. They still had one lens intact when she had found them but the lens gave her a headache so she'd forced it out. Her new favourite show, having grown out of *Button Moon*, was *Going Round the Twist*, a children's series that followed the Twist family through mysterious hauntings after moving into an old lighthouse. From the first episode, Steph was hooked and insisted that she too, would discover strange things about old buildings. So her fascination with Weasendale House was born. Yvonne never saw harm in it as Steph was so passionate about her findings and it encouraged her to use her imagination and spend time away from the television.

Eager to get on with her 'investigations', Steph planted a kiss gently on Mervyn's cheek and promised to talk more when she had finished 'working' and darted out of her grandfather's bedroom. Being as quick as she was, she had not noticed that his speech was lessoning and his tremor had worsened. Yvonne did and it was probably a good thing that Stephanie was too young and eager to get started with her game to notice. It was the first time in months that she had not made her way into Mary's room to greet her, she simply ran past at high speed to make her way to the quietest part of the building at the back, not far from the door which led to the basement. She past Mary's door so quick in fact, that she did not notice it was wide open and empty.

*****

As her feet pounded on the ground, all she could hear was the sound of her heart beat racing beneath her clothes, hammering through her small frame. She was trying to get to where she knew was the creepiest, well hidden part of the building where she would not be disturbed and would be able to get her notepad out and jot down her make-believe notes on the history of the house. No doubt her findings would consist of fairies and goblins which seemed to be her favourite supernatural entities to date. It was not likely that Steph knew much about ghosts this early into her life, any experiences she may have had would have gone unrecognised.

She stopped running as soon as she reached the furthest side of the house, without any windows and being on the North side it was shaded and felt a little colder than elsewhere. Steph soon wished she had her jacket on. She lumped herself down the wall and onto the floor. The carpet was a deep mahogany-colour that clashed against her skinny white legs that rested on it. She pulled out her notebook and pen from the small dog-shaped rucksack she had on her back and jotted down a few irrelevant observations, believing that they would lead her to discover some magical mystery hidden within the walls of the old house.

She hummed a tuned to herself that she had heard on the radio in the dining room. "Steph? Steph?" a voice called from the opposite side of the hall; behind the small wooden door that led to the basement.

She froze, "Steph, is that you? I'm locked down here. I can't get out." A familiar voice explained. "I think the nurses shut me down here, it's Mary. Can you help me get out?"

The child pushed herself to her feet and slowly stepped across the corridor to the basement. She thought back to all of the times that her Mum had forbidden her from opening the door and going down there, *it's dark and very dangerous*, she had warned. Steph was not a rule breaker and always did as she was told but surely this time she would be allowed to go against her mother's warning as there was an adult trapped down there needing help.

"Mary?" she called out, waiting for the familiar voice to reply to her, as she reached out and turned the brass knob. "Mary, is that you?"

The door opened, it wasn't locked like it had been the few times Steph had tried to investigate before. Maybe they'd gotten rid of any danger and it was safe for her to go down. She stretched round and slid the rucksack from her back and took out the small torch she'd bought with her, knowing it might come in handy for her 'investigations'.

Only the top five steps leading down into the basement were visible, the shadows had devoured the ones that followed. The walls were coated in cobwebs and a dust that seemed to have settled many years before, shielding the colour of the bricks beneath it. She took her eyes from what lay ahead of her for just a moment to look down to find the switch on the torch. She had to use both of her thumbs to force it to the ON position. Instantly the light forced its way through the clog of dust that fell through the air like tiny moths infesting her breathing. She had to raise her hand to her face to shield it from the coating of cobwebs that were trying to rest on her skin. Her eyes scattered through her surroundings as she slowly made her way further into the forbidden basement.

"Mary? It's Steph, are you OK?" Her tiny voice was consumed by the vast space around her. "Are you there?"

There was not a reply. Only silence. When she made it to the bottom of the steps, she levelled both of her feet onto the concrete ground. It looked dirty and she noticed puddles scattered throughout that she knew she must avoid else her Mum would know she had been somewhere she should not. She shone the torch in a full three-sixty circle. The basement appeared empty besides the enormous amount of clinical equipment, old bed frames and other odd pieces of rusty equipment. As she flicked the torch past the far corner of the room she noticed something sparkle in the light, hanging on the back of a bed post. She looked around quickly to make sure she was not being watched, no one had followed her, and then made her way over to the treasure she thought she had found as fast as her feet would take her. It was a beautiful gold chain with a pretty pink lily pendant that hung over the edge of the metal frame. It was swinging when she approached it, but naïve as she was, Steph did not so much as ask herself why. She picked up the piece and examined it for a while.

"It's for you," came a voice from the other side of the room she had just run from, "I want you to have it."

Steph stood with the necklace dangling between her small fingers, swinging it back and forth as her attention turned to whoever it was that was speaking to her from the darkness.

"Mary, is that you?" she asked but this time, there was no reply. "Mary?" she whispered amongst the shadows.

She waited but no one answered her. She rubbed her arms vigorously with her clammy hand, whilst the other held on tightly to her torch. It was much colder beneath the building than what it was in the house. The torch light flickered. Still unable to see who it was, but with curiosity overwhelming her sense of fear, she crept forward further, waving the torch as far out in front of her body as she could.

That is one great thing about children; impulse. They do not have the instinct to fear or doubt; if they had never been frightened, they would not know how to apprehend such situations. Steph was only able to imagine that the voice she could hear was Mary and that she was, for one reason or another, hiding.

"Do you want to come upstairs with me, Mary? I'm investigating the Weasendale ghosts," she asked as she loosened her step and started on her way towards the stairs.

When she reached the bottom, she took one last look around; the yellowing beam of the light pressing against the dark brick walls, nothing obstructing them. There was no one down there and for the first time, Steph realised that she was alone and it could not have been Mary she was speaking to. Feeling a prickle along her spine, she turned on her heel and jumped up every step, pushing as hard as she could with every muscle until she threw herself through the basement door and onto the comfort of the familiar carpet in the corridor. She scrambled her way from her knees back to her feet, as she ran the length of the hall. She stopped at the swinging door which divided the back of the house with the front. She looked behind her, back down the darkened corridor and could see the edge of the basement door still open.

A sense of dread come over her, panicking that she might get caught, she had to go back and shut the door else someone would know she had been down there. No one would believe that Mary had lured her down, and if it had not been Mary, then it must have been another adult in the home tricking her. Either way she knew she must cover her tracks. She moved slowly this time, nervous that she might get caught but more concerned about what, or who was down in the basement.

Creeping slowly, Steph heard a noise coming from up ahead; it sounded like someone was crying. This time she stopped, she was not going to be fooled again. Standing on the spot, she waited; for what, she wasn't sure. The crying stopped and so she continued to retrace her tracks back along the corridor, all the time watching the door at the end of the long, narrow hallway. She never noticed how dark it was before, and how far she was from the rest of the house. Suddenly the basement door moved, ever so slightly, further open. She stopped again, feeling a wind blow into her, a gale so strong that it knocked her to the floor and as it did, the door to the basement slammed shut. Stephanie jumped to her feet and ran as fast as her skinny legs would take her, all the way back to her grandfather's bedroom, where her Mum was still arranging his outfit for the day.

"Are you OK, sweetheart," Yvonne asked as Steph threw her arms around her mother's waist. "Did you hear about Mary?"

Steph looked up at her Mum, confused.

"Mary passed away last night sweetheart," Yvonne explained, "she fell asleep and the angels came and took her. She's with Nanny now," Yvonne explained in the kindest way she could.

Stephanie's eyes drowned in tears as she tasted the salty drops that fell along her skin and dripped from her chin. *How could she be dead?* She asked herself, *I've just seen her.*

But she had not seen her; she had not seen anyone.

Chapter thirteen. Six feet under.

1990 was a colourful year when neon tights were all the rage. Thatcher had kept her title in power and Rick Astley was still in the charts. Stephanie turned seven in the October. She celebrated with family and friends and wore her favourite Teenage Mutant Ninja Turtle tracksuit.

Jane, now nineteen and just split from a long-term relationship was usually out with friends, partying and imitating Madonna in the best way she knew how. She had the entire *Like a Virgin* dance routine finely tuned and was always the queen of the dance-floor. Although Yvonne was always there for her, she did not interfere with Jane's social life too much. The teen tantrums continued longer than usual and so she would chose to turn a blind eye to the aluminous pink tights and fish net gloves.

It had become obvious to both Eric and Yvonne that there was something a little 'special' about Stephanie. Not 'special' academically or socially, but something that perhaps had been passed down to her by her late grandfather. She could have only been five or six when on a glorious day she had taken a plate up the back garden and had been playing for some time, too much time probably, making mud cakes. She often did this and then offered them out to those willing to play along with the hideous game. But this particular day she had left the plate and plastic bowl by the back door, her mum and sister watching her from the kitchen as she made her way up the three steps from the patio to the lawn.

"What do you think she's doing?" Jane asked as she kept a watchful eye on her little sister's movements.

"I wouldn't worry, you know what she's like; her imagination's all over the place," Yvonne said as she sliced through an overly ripe tomato; the seeds bursting through the skin like lava from a volcano. "Damn it!" she cursed as she looked down at her white blouse that was now splattered with tomato juice.

Jane did not move, she just stood, watching.

Steph was now down on her knees, leaning onto her palms with her ear pressed against the grass; her fingers itching at the surface. As Jane observed, she noticed that her little sister's mouth was moving, like she was speaking or whispering to someone but she was alone in the garden.

"She looks crazy," Jane said, turning to face Yvonne who was still mopping herself clean.

"Leave her alone, she's fine," Yvonne dismissed Jane's concern, "can you pass me the cucumbers before I cook something else entirely."

The women busied themselves in the kitchen. Eric was busying himself in the lounge by watching three different football matches on the television at the same time. A skill he had mastered over the years of being an avid sportsman, both on and off the field. Completely oblivious to what his daughter was up to, he continued to curse at the players for missing a goal or their big opportunity. He would have had money at stake no doubt.

Stephanie made a very sudden entrance into the lounge through the open patio doors.

"Everything OK?" Eric asked without taking his eyes from the box, another skill he had picked up, to react without actually having a clue what's going on.

"Jane! Jane!" Steph screamed, as she came to a halt on the cold, tiled floor in the kitchen. "Jane, come with me, I need to show you something."

"I won't be a minute, Mum," Jane said as she tried to hide the fact that her little sister was coated in mud. "What on earth have you been doing, Steph?"

"Come with me, I'll show you," Steph wiped a tear that was dribbling down her cheek.

The two girls walked through the lounge and into the garden, leaving their shoes at the door. Whatever it was that Steph had to share, was obviously important.

"There's a little girl in there," Steph said, pointing at the hole she had just spent the past five minutes digging, "she's buried in there and she can't get out." She looked at Jane, whose attention was on the mound of mud in front of her, "can you get her out?"

Jane said nothing, and instead sat herself down on the floor. Steph copied her. "Why would you say such a thing, Steph? How would you think this one up?"

"I haven't, I promise!" Steph replied, tearfully. "She said that she is lost and needs to get out so she can find her Mummy. Please help her."

Steph spoke with such trauma that Jane could not help but believe her; that and the fact that her fingernails were full with damp mud and cuts that her little sister was completely oblivious to. "I'll speak to Mum," Jane agreed, as she coaxed her sister back inside to make some cookies for tea, they would surely taste better than the mud cakes she had been handing out.

*****

It was later that evening, when Steph had gone to bed, that Jane told Yvonne what had happened that afternoon. Instantly Yvonne remembered what she had been told all those years ago about the farm fire and the children who had been killed. About the fireplace that was once reconstructed with the grave of a child behind it; a young girl. A chill ran through her.

"I wouldn't worry, Jane, you know what an imagination that girl has. Don't let her pull you in to her fantasy world." Yvonne smiled as she leant forward and kissed her daughter on her forehead, trying to hide the fear that resided in her voice as it trembled.

113

*****

Yvonne suggested to Jane not to mention what had happened in the garden anymore to Steph for the time being. If it was something they could try to ignore, then she thought it might be best to do exactly that. She mentioned it to Eric that night.

"She may take after Dick, you think?" She had asked, "She could have the same abilities your father had."

"Dad did everything he could to encourage his 'abilities' and I doubt that Steph knows enough about what you say she's doing to be encouraging them. It's unlikely that these things would just happen to a little girl, surely?"

But of course Yvonne knew more of the houses' history than she had ever let on to her husband, if only because her curiosity over the years had gotten the better of her. That, and because Eric did his best to distance himself from the place, but she thought it was, at least, possible that Steph had inherited some of Richard's sensitivity to the paranormal.

*****

The following morning Yvonne gave Steph the option of staying at home with her father, who no doubt would spend his time watching football; or she could go shopping with her and Jane, dropping in on Granddad on their way home. Steph chose the latter. As they were heading out of Hertfordshire for the trip, Yvonne allowed her to take her keyboard. It was only the plastic type that had the demo tunes on auto-touch (that drove everyone crazy) but she was pretty good at it and was able to recall most melodies by ear so Yvonne encouraged her to play. It was another similarity she shared with her late grandfather.

114

They were headed to a large shopping centre only thirty minutes from where they lived, and the sun was pounding in through the windows so they had no choice but to keep them down for some ventilation in the stifling car. Unfortunately they spent fifteen minutes breathing in the stink from the smoke that was chugging out of the Ford in front of them. Chris Tarrant was chatting on the radio about the latest music news that neither Jane nor Yvonne paid much attention too. Jane only tuned in when a track came on the station that she recognised. She would turn the volume up and join in with the lyrics she knew. Steph would join in too even though she did not know the words and Yvonne just smiled with contentment, enjoying the sound of her daughters' voices.

Hearing Spandau Ballet come through the speakers, Jane turned down the volume; she was not keen on ballads, she hated anything remotely lovey-dovey. With the radio down, Steph turned on her keyboard and pressed the button three times to the all-familiar tune, *BINGO Was His Name.*

Jane tutted, "Mum, tell her to stop. I don't think I can bear to listen to this anymore today, it's driving me insane."

A smile crept across Yvonne's face, "Steph, sweetheart, isn't there something you can play us? Make something up for us."

Steph turned off the monotonous tune and sat still for a moment. The traffic started to clear so Yvonne turned the engine back on and pushed into second gear for the third time in almost thirty minutes.

"Thank God," Jane took her feet off the glove box and pushed them back into her pumps that were hiding beneath her seat.

Whilst she had her head between her knees, tying up her laces, Yvonne turned the radio off completely and took her foot off the accelerator, indicating into the slow lane. Jane sat up and looked round at her Mum who was now cruising at fifty. Yvonne looked round at Steph who was playing the notes of a familiar tune.

"Mum, that sounds like …"

"It is," Yvonne answered before Jane had time to finish, "it's impossible."

Both women sat for a while, listening to the seven year old girl who was sitting in the back of their car playing a song that her grandfather had written more than six years before she was born. A song that he played to Jane when she was about the same age as Steph. Richard was a musician, a pianist who played by memory, never by song sheets which made writing music easy. When he met Ellen, he spent a lot of his free time (which was not often) playing his own music, always by memory. No one would have been able to learn what he played, especially if they had not been born at the time. The piece Steph was playing was called, *Happiness*, he always told Jane that he felt like playing it when she was around. She had always loved that.

"Steph, where did you hear that song?" Yvonne asked, slowing the car down further and glancing over her shoulder to watch her daughter's reaction.

Steph stopped playing. "I didn't Mummy, I made it up like you said," her eyes beaming through Yvonne's, full of honesty and truth.

She's not lying, Yvonne thought.

"It's a lovely song," Jane said, "play us another."

Yvonne nudged Jane's leg, not wanting to encourage her. Steph looked down at her keyboard once again and raised her tiny index finger to her lip whilst she was clearly thinking of what to play next.

She started off slow but as the pace built, so the melody became recognisable. *Daisy, Daisy*.

"Didn't Granddad…"

"Shhhhhhh," Yvonne insisted, whilst nodding her head.

It was possible that Steph had heard *Daisy, Daisy* from friends, at school or even on one of the kids programs she

116

watched, but that was not the analogy that Yvonne had. *Daisy, Daisy* was her mother's favourite song and one that she had always ask Dick to play if ever the families had a get together.

"Strange child," Jane said as she turned herself back around as they slowly approached their turn off.

A coincidence it could have been but all the same, Yvonne kept the radio off to reminisce on the memorable notes that her daughter played.

*****

Stephanie had always been different from other children, probably not noticeably to those who were not close to her or the family, but to anyone who was around her long enough to pick out the finer details. Shortly before Stephanie's eighth birthday, Jane had started dating and was onto her second serious relationship—a guy called Pete. He went to the boys' high school in Bishop's Stortford and had an army of girls swooning over his lavish good looks and long blonde hair; he was an epitome of the eighties. Jane's parents had old fashioned values; the correct morals in many eyes—strict morals in others—but should Pete want to sleep over, then he would have to take the sofa. Jane preferred having the bed to herself anyway so it suited her just fine.

They had been out with friends, Jane's curfew was midnight; she was nineteen and was being accompanied home by a man who both Yvonne and Eric liked. They fell through the door, both telling each other to keep quiet, "Shhhhhhh, you'll wake my parents up," Jane giggled, not realising that Yvonne was already awake.

Although Yvonne never grew up drinking or going to heavy raves, she was not naïve and was well aware of the things that kids got up to and she considered herself blessed she was not bringing them up in the sixties.

117

The two teens kissed briefly before Jane grabbed a bottle of lemonade from the fridge and took it with her upstairs to bed. Pete had himself a glass of water and settled down, fully dressed underneath a duvet which Yvonne had left out for him at the end of the vibrantly patterned sofa. The fabric moved in his vision as though he was dancing in a still room; it made his head hurt if he looked at it for too long. He closed his eyes to avoid the room from spinning more than necessary and hopefully prevent him from throwing up; and began to drift into a shallow sleep.

He watched as he saw himself in a house, not too dissimilar to his own, but one which had deep red roses leading to its door. Roses that were damp with the humid air, damp with a sticky red substance that he only realised was blood when he reached out and touched one of the petals and it left a residue on his index finger. As he stroked the velvet-soft petal, he had the urge to tug at it, pulling it free from its restraints but as he did, the flower bit him, taking off his entire finger and causing his own screams to wake him.

He sat upright on the sofa and after realising where he was, he settled back into his pillow, hoping that his cries did not wake anyone else in the house. The room was dark and he was pleased that it was not spinning as much as before. His mouth felt dry like he had been sucking on leather so he reached down the side of the sofa, where he had earlier rested his glass. It was dark, so he was not able to see properly and was a little worried he might knock the water over onto the carpet that lay beneath it. He decided he would stand up and turn on the lamp that was behind him but as he swung his arm back, it hit something about mid-way up—something or someone. He pulled his arm back in and pushed himself into a seated position against the back cushion.

"Hello?" He asked into the darkness.

No one answered. *You're still drunk you silly sod,* he sniggered at the thought of his reaction. He climbed off the sofa and walked over to the main light switch. It was on a dimmer so he turned it down low before pressing it 'on'. "Oh my…! Steph!" he exclaimed whilst analysing the small child that stood in front of him.

Initially he thought she was sleeping, a majority of children would sleep walk and he presumed this was what Steph was doing but as he approached her, she turned to face him.

"She was watching you before I was here," she told him, "the little girl that I see in my dreams. She likes you," she said, watching, waiting for a reaction from him, but Pete just stood motionless, considering the likelihood that he was still intoxicated from the sambuca and tequila he had been knocking back all night.

"You should be in bed, Steph, what are you doing down here, watching me? Let me take you back to bed," he held out his hand to her.

"I wasn't watching you," she replied, "I was watching her."

She pointed to the far end of the sofa that would have been where Pete's feet had been poking out the end of the duvet. The space was empty but it was enough to send a chill down his spine.

"Come on you," he said as he lifted her into his arms, "let's get you back to bed."

*****

Steph had never sleepwalked before or after that night, but when Pete had explained the disturbances he had in the night to Jane the following morning, she laughed and said that she must have been. Pete was not convinced. He drove home that morning trying his very best not think any more about Jane's creepy little sister.

119

*****

It sounds odd to anyone who has not experienced anything paranormal, but for those who do, the small things become second nature; you learn to live with them. Like money going missing and turning up where you would have looked fifteen minutes before ransacking your entire house; like the sound of footsteps upstairs when your entire family is downstairs; and like your small daughter talking to people who you can only hope are imaginary friends.

But there are some things, however, that you cannot ever get used to.

Chapter fourteen. Movie trailers.

The age gap between the two girls had its advantages, Jane was a live-in babysitter. Yvonne and Eric did not arrange much without the children but they did enjoy a meal out every once in a while and it was in August 1991 that Eric wanted to take Yvonne to their favourite Chinese restaurant in the small town where they lived. Jane sometimes complained about having to stay home on a weekend but she did not have any plans and was not particularly put-out, so she agreed without much fuss.

"We shouldn't be back late," Yvonne told Steph, as she made her way about her bedroom, picking up a pearl necklace from her dresser and adding it to the outfit she was wearing, "you be a good girl for Jane."

Steph was sitting on the edge of her bed, watching her Mum get ready and making herself look glam. Steph was such a tomboy that she could not imagine why anyone would want to dress up in dresses and cover their faces in make-up, but no doubt her opinions would eventually change. Boys were still only useful for helping her climb trees and going on bike rides. Her best friend was a little boy who lived opposite her, his name was Andrew. He was the sort of boy who found it tough to make friends, with red hair and a little pot belly that was no doubt filled with biscuits and cakes he had made at Scouts, but Steph appreciated his silly humour and adventurous personality so they were inseparable.

"Can I play out with Andrew for a while before dinner please, Mum?" Steph asked as she jumped up at the bedroom window, looking to see if her friends were still riding their bikes outside.

Despite Greenmay Close being a quiet cul-de-sac, Yvonne was always apprehensive about letting Stephanie play outdoors, but she trusted her to stick to the pavements and not go out of sight of the house.

"Is Elizabeth still outside?" Yvonne asked, pursing her lips and coating them in Velvet Cherry. Elizabeth was the little girl who lived next door, a quiet girl, three years older than Steph, and a good friend who Yvonne trusted to look out for her. "OK, but I want you in by seven o'clock; Jane's cooking you dinner."

Jane was not cooking her dinner; if she did, it would be about as edible as a sandwich made of Playdough. Yvonne had tried over the years to rub her culinary skills onto to her eldest but to no avail and she had given up trying. By 'cooking dinner' what she actually meant was that she would reheat something that Yvonne had prepared earlier for them.

"Jane's got some Crusha milkshake mix for dessert to make if you eat dinner, OK?"

"Great!" Steph proclaimed as she ran out her parent's bedroom, and down the stairs to the entrance hall.

Even though the road was safe, Yvonne still worried about her eight-year-old daughter playing outside. In the eighties it was not child molesters and paedophiles you needed to be concerned with, it was the careless drivers who might not realise that children were playing on those quiet roads. In the eighties, no one assumed that such scumbags existed.

Yvonne and Eric finished getting themselves ready, Yvonne made more of an effort than her husband, although she need not have done as she was equally as beautiful with or without makeup. She hurried around, sorting out the girls, and finally made it out the door, calling to Steph and telling her to hurry inside just as soon as Jane told her to.

It was not long before dusk, that Jane remembered her little sister was outside. She had her head buried in a Stephen King novel. She had almost every book he had ever written proudly displayed in her bedroom and she had read each one more than once. She was a fast reader, reading a book a day which was great for college work. Her homework was always done before most of her friends had even looked at it. She put the book down on the dining table, which was already laid for dinner, with the cover page spread open devouring a small paper boat and a drain on the front.

"Steph, dinners burnt!" Jane yelled from the door, and she was not joking either. She had somehow managed to burn a meal that she had not even prepared, although Steph did not complain. She loved her big sister to bits and would probably eat dog muck if Jane said it was OK to do so.

They cleared the table and spent the following half an hour making chocolate milkshake, which took equally as long to clean up the mess from shaking half the contents of it all over the kitchen worktops. Cheap milkshake shakers were a disaster waiting to happen, but for the girls making a mess was part of the fun. A bit like eating more of the cake mixture than the finished product, the Camp sisters were victims of that as well.

It was around eight o'clock when Jane told Steph to get ready for bed. She was not your usual, bossy older sibling and she had no intention of sending her little sister to bed (if she had of done she knew that Steph would only hide underneath her duvet with a copy of one of her horror novels, attempting to sound out words like *gruesome* and *savagery),* she was better off staying up with her. Plus, Jane loved the company. By the time Steph made her way back downstairs, Jane had already planned to watch *Children of the Corn.* She knew full-well Steph was not allowed to watch it but did not see much harm in her sitting through the trailers.

Steph was not your typical eight year-old, she was wise before her time and was not as naïve as some other kids her age. Jane knew that when her copy of *It* or *Salam's Lot* went missing, it would be likely she would find her little

123

sister hiding in a den she had made, somewhere in the house, torch in hand, forcing her way through vocabulary she was actually clueless about just because she loved the horror hidden within a book's pages. Steph did not know much about her late grandfather but the similarities were uncanny—not in the physical sense, obviously, but her interests and fascinations. She did not know about her Granddad Dick's past, it was not something a parent could drop into a conversation with a young child, *and by the way, your grandfather, whom's birthday you share, was a medium.* Not just because she was too young to be accustomed with such things, in the contrary; she already knew too much.

It was the third trailer that Steph saw him. His skin reminded her of a picture she had seen once of the Everglades taken from such a height that it looked like tunnels running through a forest; uneven and ridged. His nose was long and eyes narrow, like slits in a pie and the pastry was raw. He wore a dirty, black hat that only a star in an old John Wayne movie might be proud of and a jumper of a completely different calibre. The worst thing, what Steph could not comprehend, was that Freddie had knives instead of fingers. The shiny blades glistened in the light as the camera panned across his character. He was utterly terrifying. Steph had seen the dead walking, ghosts haunting and clowns with oversized grins and fangs like sharks teeth; blood, guts, it was all the same, she had seen worse in her school playground. And yet, she had never been so enticed but yet utterly terrified of a character in all her life.

Jane looked round at her smaller sister, who had squashed herself into the far corner of the sofa, a cushion rammed into her stomach, eyes fixed on the screen.

"Steph, maybe you should go to bed now, Mum would go crazy at me if she knew I'd let you see this." Jane said, flooded with guilt that her sister looked petrified. "Come on, let's go up and have a look at that book you picked up from school." Steph fidgeted in her seat and shifted her concentration from the ugly monster on the television screen to her beautiful sister. "Come on," Jane said, grabbing hold of the cushion that Steph was still clinging to, "get yourself up to bed, I'll be up in a minute."

Steph jumped up, probably already forgotten about the man wearing the striped sweater and knives instead of a hand; probably.

Jane turned her attention back to the television which she had paused on a frame of a girl being dragged across the ceiling. *Idiot,* she cursed as even she cringed at the image. She could only imagine what Steph must have felt. She intended to read a little longer with her than usual that night.

*****

Jane stayed upstairs with Steph until she fell asleep. She never really knew whether or not Steph was actually asleep or whether she was pretending so that she could sneak on the television or read a book. She took herself back downstairs and returned her attention to the movie she had intended to watch.

Steph waited until she heard Jane take the twelfth stair and then shifted position. Tonight she did not feel like watching TV or reading about more gruesome tales than she already had flashing in her mind like a rated eighteen version of a View Master. She tried to remind her imagination that she was safe and at home in bed, a million miles from the child killer she had been introduced to earlier that evening. She stretched her lower limbs as she turned to face the wall. She slept in a cabin bed, so she was up high, about two foot from the ceiling with a desk and wardrobe beneath her. She did not have to ask more than once before her parents agreed it was a great storage saving

125

idea and got a white one delivered to match the rest of the furniture in her room. She started to think about school and what she would be doing in gymnastics the following week, avoiding all re-acquaintance with that horrible man in the movie, and found herself drifting to sleep.

*****

Due to an over-active imagination, Steph found it almost impossible to sleep without dreaming. Usually she was blessed with dreams of her family, holidays and pets. The typical dreams of a young girl. But sometimes, occasionally, she was plagued by nightmares. Not the type that incurred spiders or critters hiding under the bed, but ones which left her heart racing and tears streaming down her cheeks. She had often woken her parents up by screaming that she was going to be swallowed whole by her bedroom, and that she would be eaten by the furniture in her room and that no one would be able to find her. It was an odd night-terror that her parents would blame on her age and imagination, but tonight the nightmare was of him. He had found her hiding in her bed. She reached everywhere to find her torch, to help give her some chance of getting away but as her hands scurried through the duvet it was filled with a warm mush that she squeezed through her fingertips and as she tried to pull her hands away and push herself up, they sunk into the mattress which had also become a puddle of slop. Her body began to sink and as it did, she could hear him laughing as her body was consumed by the innards of his previous victim.

*****

This time she did not wake screaming, but as she threw herself into a seated position, her heart pounding so hard it felt as though it would push right through her ribs, breaking each one of them as it did; she felt something touch the back of her head. She touched her hair but there was nothing there. The room was darker, much darker than it had been when she fell asleep, which must have been a few hours earlier. Her bedroom door was on ajar, as Jane had left it and she could see that her parent's door was closed which meant they must be home and in bed. She laid herself back down, thinking that it must have been another night terror. Over the years she had began to get used to them. She settled herself under the duvet and as she did, she pushed her thumb into the palm of her hand and wrapped her fingers around it. This was something she'd read about in some comic book she had picked up at car-boot sale about witchcraft and wizardry. It was supposed to ward off evil spirits and protect you. Whether or not it actually worked was another matter altogether. She knew about Voodoo Dolls and this worked in the same way and whether or not there was truth in it, it always seemed to psychologically convince Steph that she was safe. She felt something soggy behind the crease of her index finger; she rolled it between her fingers for a moment or two and then reached under the mattress for the torch she always had hiding under there. She leant on her elbows and twisted the torch on and directed the light onto to her hand so that she could examine what the soft tissue was that she had felt there. As she inspected it, she found a red pulp that was splattered sporadically across her right hand, the type of mess you might see if you had been cooking with mincemeat; a warm gooey matter that had transported from her dream.

She pushed and scrambled her way up, kicking the duvet off of her clammy bare legs. She wiped the splatter from her hand along the side of her mattress which was wedged against the bed-frame, she would clean it off tomorrow. She picked up the torch which she had thrown down by her feet, the beam still pushing through the darkness as she waved it around the empty room. She was alone, there was nothing to be afraid of as she settled herself back down, lying on her back, trying to think about anything but what had just happened.

Holding the torch below her chin with both hands cupped around it, she flicked the switch on and off at the ceiling, creating an SOS for no-one but herself to see. As she concentrated, she felt her eyelids become heavy and she begun to drift back into her subconscious where, no doubt, she would be greeted with both nightmares and dreams.

Back in reality, she heard a scratching sound, like someone tearing thin paper in front of her face; it was coming from above her. She opened her eyes and looked up at the ceiling. There was a dim light pushing its way through the creases in the curtains and her eyes soon adjusted. Everything seemed normal so she closed her eyes again. She could feel her heart beat pushing through her nightie, lifting her chest up and down - up and down – trying to control her breathing and reassuring her innocent mind. The sound remained, this time much louder, like finger nails down a black-board. She opened her eyes wide, bulging and without the speed or ability to move quick enough before it could strike, the ceiling split open, and a shining blade edged its way through, ripping the plaster further apart and pushing closer to Stephanie's face. Fear froze her body, she opened her mouth to scream but nothing would come out. She grabbed onto the ledge of the bed and without thinking, threw herself over the edge, avoiding the wafer thin blades by no more than a few centimetres. She landed on her knees on the floor with a thud, twisting her wrist as she fell.

She did not look back, she did not need reassurance that what she had seen was real. She ran past her parents' bedroom door which was closed and considered running into her sister's room when she saw that the light downstairs was on. *It must be Dad,* she thought and legged it down the stairs as quick as a child running through their favourite park. She spun the corner and ran straight ahead into the lounge; the light was dimmed but she could see the reflective shadows on the wall that the television made. Expecting to find her Dad awake or asleep in his favourite armchair, she already felt her nerves calm but when she entered the room, it was empty, no one was in there. The television was on and before she crept round the back of the armchair she could hear that terrible screech; the one that puts your nerves on edge and that makes the hairs on the back of your neck stand on end, metal against board; metal tearing its way through plaster, teasing its way through your mind. She did not need to look, she did not need to see with her eyes what she already knew was on the television, playing and replaying, she was already scared witless as she forcefully heard the screeching of his metal fingers, scratching against a surface as kids screamed for their lives in the background. It was the film of which she had watched the trailer of earlier on, the man from her nightmare was acting out one of his violent murders. She ran back from where she came from and before bursting into her parents' bedroom, she briefly looked into her own bedroom. There was no one there and no sign of any disturbance or evidence of what she had experienced. The ceiling was clear of any damage, her torch light was still studying the back wall as it lay on its side on the carpet. She burst into her parent's bedroom; she jumped into the middle of their bed.

"Steph, what's wrong?" Yvonne asked as she felt her daughter's tiny body shaking next to her.

"Just a bad dream, Mum," she replied, pushing her face into her mother's back, "go back to sleep, I can sleep fine here."

Eric turned his back and continued to snore quietly, the sound comforting to Steph's ears, her parent's warm bodies soothing her fear.

She knew what just happened could not possibly be real. It was impossible that the man with the knives could come out of a movie and into her home. Something else could make it seem like he had, but she could not imagine who or what would want to scare her so badly.

Chapter fifteen. No lives spared.

Steph chose not to share the experience she had with anyone unless she really had to. She knew that her parents would believe her, they did about most other things, but more than anything she did not want to worry them. Yvonne spent half her time worrying about Mervyn and Eric was busy with work. Compared to other children her age, she was pretty clued-up on things and had convinced herself that the horror movie she had seen a glimpse of had developed in her overactive imagination.

*****

It was when the leaves began to fall in the same way that the temperature did, that Mervyn's Parkinson's disease seemed to develop quite suddenly. His speech had deteriorated over the years, a side effect of the drugs more than the disease, and what would grate on Yvonne's nerves more than anything else was people's obnoxious behaviour when it came to the disease. Being fairly uncommon, those that did not have personal experience of it, would sometimes presume Mervyn was an alcoholic. Pretty naïve considering that his symptoms were nothing like those shown in the latter. Whenever Yvonne took him out for lunch the waitress would always address her, "And what would he like to have?" they would ask in the politest manner they could muster.

"I'm not sure, he's sitting there so why don't you ask him," would always be her reply, often *tutting* under her breath and repeating the question to her father who would sometimes struggle to answer in any hurry but who would always manage to reply.

That is something you learn in life. No one ever seems to have enough time or patience.

One sunny September morning, Yvonne had arranged to take a small group from Weasendale House on a trip to a coastal town in Essex called Southend. She had taken them before and everyone who had accompanied her on her last trip was extremely enthusiastic about returning. The home hired and paid for a minibus and off Yvonne went, like something out of a *Carry On* movie minus the big boobs and, hopefully, the mishaps.

*****

Mervyn loved spending time with his daughter regardless of what they were doing and he appreciated the effort that she went to at making his last few years easier. The disease seemed to hit so much harder when he lost Elsie. She was such a huge part of his life that without her, everything became difficult. They had met when they were just sixteen, at a dance that neither one of them usually cared for but were forever grateful that they both went. They married young, had children soon after but never lost sight of the love they shared. Mervyn never greeted his wife without a 'darling' or a 'sweetheart', and he never found a bad word to say about her. He carried much of the old fashioned respect that men once had for women, some still do but most would not recognise it even if it slapped them across the face.

When the doctor told Mervyn that he had Parkinson's disease, it was not a great shame as no one really knew what the disease was. Yvonne had taken herself straight to the library where she found out about the symptoms (shaking, memory loss, slurred speech) and had briefly told Elsie, but her Mum was not around to see many of the symptoms progress. Whilst she was alive, the medication he took seemed to control it, but no amount of pill popping could cure his symptoms. Yvonne spoke to his doctor aside from his usual meetings and he confirmed that stress and emotional loss could cause rapid progression.

The loss of Elsie had accelerated the progression of his symptoms, and then losing Mary too seemed to have made things worse. Being at Weasendale House helped a great deal. Yvonne's love and patience was precious and he would be forever grateful. Not everyone would be as lucky as he was. He had always been a particularly self-sufficient, intelligent man who had fought in the war and seen more good men killed than a doctor in an emergency unit. In his early years, he had worked his way from tea boy to President of a company which juggled money and paid its way through the economy.

When he was diagnosed with a disease he knew nothing about, it was hard to accept. He felt like a child being told they had to go to school, whether they liked it or not; he had to deal with the disease as it progressed through its ugly stages. The fact that Elsie was no longer with him to hold his hand and to make life more bearable was hard but it would have been more difficult if he did not have his kind-hearted daughter.

*****

They did their usual routine of walking along the pebble beach. There was an ice-cream stop thrown in about half way down where the elderly would enjoy laughing at each other's ability to smother their faces in the sticky, cold mess. Yvonne would never be too far away with a wet-wipe to sort them out.

They were standing outside a small franchise shop of Wimpy when Mervyn first said that he was not feeling well. The colour had drained from his face, like a sand picture being cleared from an Etcha-Sketch.

"Dad! Are you OK?" Yvonne's face was full of concern, "You look so pale."

133

"No love, I don't think I am. Can we go home?"

He did not have to ask twice. Yvonne made everyone finish or throw the remainder of their batter covered fish and escorted them all quickly onto the minibus.

*****

It turned out that Mervyn had a mini stroke and it was lucky that Yvonne had been quick to read the signs. He spent several weeks in hospital and the effect the stroke had on his disease was devastating. It encouraged his symptoms, forcing his doctors to up the dosage of his medication and ultimately prevent him from living his life as well as he had been. Since Mary's death, he had returned to the quiet man he had been before he met her and now that his symptoms had developed, his speech and movement was impaired, forcing him to withdraw from group activities.

There were days when he would not recognise Yvonne or his grandchildren, and on occasion would mistake his daughter for his late wife. He was tormented by the past, the things that had happened throughout his life, both the good and the bad.

Late one Tuesday evening in November 1990, Yvonne got a call at home.

"Hi, Yvonne, sorry it's late but you should come quickly. It's your father. Maybe Eric should come and perhaps he could bring his bike," Kimberley suggested.

It was an odd request but Yvonne did as she was told and woke Eric up, "Eric, you need to get dressed," she said, nudging her husband in his side, "it's Dad, he's taken a turn for the worse."

Eric opened his eyes and pushed himself up, "What's he done? What's happened?"

"I'm not sure, but Kimberley just called and said to come quick and for you to drive your bike."

The pair of them changed and as soon as Eric pulled some trousers over his pants, he let her wake Jane, as he sped up the road on his motorbike.

When Yvonne arrived at Weasendale House, Eric's bike was not in the car park but Kimberley was there waiting for her, eager to explain what had happened. One of the nurses had noticed that Mervyn was missing from his room at about ten o'clock and after she had spent some time looking for him, she dashed into Kimberley's office to raise her cause for concern. They had searched the grounds and called the police just before she called Yvonne.

"Where's Eric?" Yvonne asked, observing the three women's faces that stood before her.

"He's out looking for him in the woods. We thought he'd be able to cover ground faster on his bike than the police can by foot," Kimberley said, grabbing her posh pink gloves from her desk, "are you ready to join the search?"

Yvonne did not have to be asked twice, and turned around and made her way into the woods, "Do you have a flash light?" She called out as the darkness prevented her from running ahead.

Before Kimberley could answer her, they heard the sweet sound of Eric's bike, speeding along the driveway towards them. He rode with Mervyn, dressed in a leather jacket and helmet, riding on the back. It was an absolute picture to see. The smile on Mervyn's face would have melted anyone's heart. When Yvonne saw her father on the back of the bike, realising he was safe and unharmed, her feet could not move her quickly enough to get over to him.

"Dad!" The joy in her voice echoed through the nurses' ears, as they watched the daughter launch herself at her father, almost knocking the bike and both men to the ground.

"He looks like bloody Evil Kenevil on the back of that thing," Kimberley said.

All three nurses shared a brief moment of hilarity.

135

*****

That night, Yvonne and the nurses at Weasendale House
were told of how Mervyn had been captured by the
Germans and that he was escaping their imprisonment. He
had described scenes that Yvonne, the nurses and Eric
could only imagine were events that happened when he
fought during the Second World War. It was as though they
had come back to haunt him years later, like a repetitive
tune that you just cannot get out of your head—trapped
there as long as your mind allows it to be.

It was the kind of story you can laugh about years later,
even when Mervyn would not be around to tell the tale,
everyone else who was there would be able to.

There was, however, a much more serious tone to what
happened that night. Mervyn had suffered such a serious
hallucination and put his life at risk that his family's nerves
were in tethers.

*****

Christmas was as eventful as always and everyone ate too
much food and drank too much port—Ellen in particular
who was still partial to a few glasses of her favourite tipple,
even though she was in her seventies. Mervyn had spent the
day at Yvonne and Eric's house and although you could not
see it in his expression because he was rattling with drugs
and the effects of the disease limited his ability to show
emotion, Yvonne caught a glint in his eye more often than
not that showed the happiness he felt on the inside to be
with his family.

Eric's birthday, New Years Eve, Yvonne had organised
for everyone to go to a local Italian restaurant to celebrate,
but at six o'clock in the morning she was woken by the
phone ringing. She moved quick, hoping that the noise

would not wake her husband who was still snoring besides her.

"Hello?" she asked into the receiver.

"Yvonne, it's Linda, you need to come now." Her voice was shaking, "Mervyn's taken a turn for the worse."

*****

Yvonne went to the home alone. She had whispered something in Eric's ear about visiting her father and had left the girls sleeping. She did not want to worry them unnecessarily and at that point she had no idea just how serious her father's condition was. But that soon became clear.

When she arrived at Weasendale House there were two nurses waiting for her outside, Beth and Sharon, women who Yvonne considered to be good friends. As she climbed out of her car, she could see by the look on both of their faces that the situation was not good, and she felt her eyes well with tears.

Kimberley was standing in Mervyn's room, by his bed side holding his hand. There was another nurse there too, Rachel, who Yvonne had also grown fond of over the years of working together.

"I'm so sorry Yvonne," Kimberley said, her eyes welling up, "but he's ready. He's holding on for you," she said as a smile briefly crept across her lips, handing Yvonne her father's hand. Yvonne looked down at her Dad whose eyes were closed, his chest raising and lowering slowly as his breathing began to soften. His mouth was slightly parted, which was likely because of the sores that had begun to appear inside. Doctors had said that they thought it was cancer growing inside him but they could not be sure. Because of his Parkinson's disease, they could not run the usual tests or offer him the treatment that he would need, Yvonne asked for her father to be allowed to savour what little time he had left without being pulled about and dosed up further on more medication.

As she held onto her father's hand, it felt cold so she pulled the duvet higher under his chin, covering a little more of his navy and white striped pajamas.

"Hi Dad," Yvonne started, her voice trembling, "I'm here now, you can go to sleep," she said as she stroked her father's forehead. For just a moment she felt his hand tighten around hers, gripping onto her fingers and all the women standing by his bedside saw a faint smile pull across his lips.

*****

Yvonne stayed at Weasendale House for a while, she had to let everything that had happened sink in. She called her brother and also Eric, both of whom made their way as fast as they could. Yvonne left her car and Eric bought her home in his, she was not in any state to drive. She could hardly string a sentence together let alone drive a car coherently. When they got home, Yvonne insisted that she be the one to tell the girls. Jane she knew was old enough and strong enough to cope with such devastating news but Steph was so young and naïve that she was worried about how she would take it.

"Let me sort myself out and then I'll tell them," Yvonne said but things never worked out as planned and as she walked through the door, Jane greeted her. She did not have to say anything, Jane was able to comprehend by the tears drowning her mother's eyes that the news must be bad.

"Steph's upstairs," Jane said, "do you want me to…"

"No, no," Yvonne interrupted, "I'll do it," she said as she moved from her daughter's embrace and made her way upstairs to Steph who she could hear playing by herself in her bedroom.

Yvonne pushed her door open gently and waited until Stephanie turned round to greet her but strangely, she did not. Yvonne watched her daughter as she finished pouring imaginary coffee into a small plastic tea cup, "Would you like one, Mum?" She asked without looking up.

"No, I'm OK thanks sweetheart," Yvonne said, moving further into the bedroom and towards her daughter, "I have something I need to tell you," she said.

Stephanie stopped what she was doing and looked up, but still not at Yvonne who was kneeling down behind her, "Is it about Granddad?" She asked, her voice strong, confident. "He just left."

Yvonne crouched motionless, behind Steph who only just began to turn to look at her mother, "Don't cry," Steph said, "Granddad is fine, he told me so, and he told me to say thank you for being there for him since Nanny died and for being there with him today when he needed you the most," Yvonne could feel all of her emotions build up inside her, her heart yearning and breaking simultaneously, "He wanted me to tell you that he's found Nanny and that everything's OK."

Yvonne could not hold back the tears any longer, and they began to flow from her eyes, down her cheeks and well on the carpet that she was still kneeling on. Steph stood up and was only a little taller than the height her mother was crouching at. She wrapped her arms around her mother's neck and laid her head on her shoulder, "It's going to be OK Mummy," she said, "Granddad feels much better now."

Chapter sixteen. A fresh start.

Being their only Grandparent left alive, Ellen spent a lot of time with the family, looking after the girls and visiting as regularly as she could. Flo had been dead for almost five years, which was a long time for Ellen to be living alone at 106 Poultney Road. You could say that she was used to it, but she was still terrified when anything untoward occurred. As with most hauntings, they did not happen all of the time, but that made it worse somehow. It was always when she least expected it that she would experience something that reminded her that she was never alone. Now that her body was aging, her movements slowing her down, she had become more vulnerable, and that was what frightened her. When Richard died it was like she had been given the key to a secret box that had been locked for a hundred years. She was curious of what resided inside her home, but now she spent her time trying to pretend that none of it was real. For years she had woken in the night, afraid of the scratching at the door and the cries she heard night after night coming from the spare rooms. Deep down she knew that she was living in a house which had been turned into a portal connecting the living with the dead.

*****

In the early hours of May 10th, 1991, Ellen was a million miles from Woodford, a million miles from humanity, as she threw back her thick, blonde hair, looking over her shoulder as she ran from Richard who was chasing her through a large open field. The sun shone brightly, she could feel the heat burn through her blouse as they laughed and she screamed out eagerly awaiting to be captured. Looking ahead of her path, she concentrated on the small gate in the distance, trying to comprehend how she would get past it without fumbling, losing footing and being caught by Richard. Although, deep down, it was the being captured that she desired. To feel his touch, smell his scent; her body longed for his embrace. Lost in her resolutions, she became aware that she was no longer able to hear Richard's laughter, his footsteps in unison with her own. She slowed down, looking behind her, no longer bothered by losing their game of kiss chase, desperate to see Richard standing there. But Richard was gone, nowhere to be seen.

Leaning forwards and resting her palms on her knees, she tried to catch her breath. "Richard?" She called into the vast countryside, "Richard, where are you?"

Her eyes darted through the landscape, behind bushes and trees, looking for any sign of life. The sun was setting, slowly from an empty sky, but up ahead Ellen could see the dark clouds, the kind that carried a storm. No sooner than she saw the blackness heading her way did she hear a clap of thunder in the distance, like a distant drum. The heavens opened and the rain belted down, drowning the tiny daisies and soaking through Ellen's blouse.

What was that? Ellen jumped around, hoping, praying that Richard would be standing before her, but the pathway was clear. It seemed as though the trees in the distance were getting closer, crowding her. She knew she could not be far from home, and she needed to be home fast. The temperature had dropped, and this time the thunder sounded as though it was overhead. She swiveled on her heels and turned to face the small wooden gate as she was before. But in front of it stood a man, dressed from head to toe in black. She felt sick, nauseated, as a putrid stench filled her nostrils. She swallowed hard, trying not to retch. She watched as the man moved towards her slowly; his long black cloak and tall black hat consumed his wafer like frame. The man slowly pulled on the rim of his hat, revealing his face hidden beneath.

Ellen took a step backwards, and then another and another until she trod on something hard and her back was wedged against something much taller than her five-foot, two-inch height. She turned quickly to see that she had somehow reached a tree, or perhaps the tree had reached her. She wanted to run, wanted to escape whatever hold this man had on her and had on her family for so many years but in every direction she turned a tree was blocking her path.

"Richard! Richard, help me!" She called, her voice screeching, pulling on her vocal cords as loud and high as she could make it.

The man in front of her got closer and had taken off his hat entirely but his face was lowered. He dropped the hat to the floor. Ellen could hear laughter, not like the fun giggles of lovers that had filled her ears not long before. This time it was menacing, like an abusive husband, watching his wife plead for his punishments to stop. Although haunting, it was vaguely familiar.

Then it hit her, she knew why she recognised the laugh, the voice that was behind it, deep and powerful, "Richard?" She said once more, but this time she said it with certainty that the man standing in front of her was the man she loved, of whom she trusted with her life, but in that moment she feared him more than anything else in the world.

"Richard, is that you?" Tears welled in her eyes as she asked the question.

The entity said nothing, and before Ellen could know for sure, before she could claim the man in front of her to be her husband, she was dragged from sleep and thrown into reality.

*****

The room was dark. Her heart was pounding and sweat was sticking to her forehead. She felt dizzy, sick, like she had eaten something bad. She wiped her clammy skin on the sleeve of her nightdress, stretching her legs out under the empty bed sheets but there was something in her way. Something or someone was restricting her movement. She asked herself whether it could be washing she had left out, but she knew that she had hung everything up that was dry. She pulled her feet back and pushed them out once more, making sure that she was not still dreaming. To her dismay, there was something heavy blocking her stretch. Her body tightened as her muscles went rigid and she pulled her knees into her chest and held her breath momentarily. But the breathing continued, in out, in out, deep, meaningful breaths. And the smell returned. That disgusting foul stench that she recognised so well from the dream, or rather, nightmare she had just woken from. Without moving, she could feel the bed sheets tugging ever so slightly, the weight that was at the end of the bed began to move higher, further up the mattress, towards her resting place. The breathing she could hear besides her own, the smell, everything intensified, building up in both Ellen's mind and senses until it was too much for her to bare. She let out her breath, threw her feet down onto the worn old carpet and ran as fast as she could from the bedroom, along the landing, down the stairs and out the front of the house. She had no idea what the time was, judging by the dim light and the sound of birds chirping, she knew it must be before five in the morning. Early but not too early to wait out on her porch until sunrise. The air was warm if she had cared but she did not. Anywhere doing anything would be better than sitting a minute longer inside that house, waiting for whoever or whatever it was that wanted to play games with her, scaring the shit out of her. She knew that no matter what she believed about Richard's spirit or about the memories that belonged inside 106 Poultney Road, her time there was over. The time had come to look for a new home.

*****

Yvonne was delighted. She thought that Ellen should leave the big old house when Richard died, but understood that Ellen had wanted to stay living there. However, now that she wanted to move, Yvonne could not be happier for her. The two women searched high and low for a small house that would be adequate for Ellen. A nice back garden, neighbours close by and a strong little community. She found her forever home in Little Paxton, Peterborough. It was a long way from Yvonne and Eric but close to where Robert lived with Janet, so Yvonne was happy for her to reside there. The day she moved in, it was like she had a film crew helping her move, everyone designated to their own tasks. The women sorted through boxes labeled, KITCHEN and ORNAMENTS, of which Ellen seemed to have no end, and the men lifted the heavy furniture. Steph was the only one left to her own devices. She took it upon herself to make sure that everywhere looked clean and had a duster and a can of polish to run over any conspicuous looking places.

The house was quaint, far from the vast space that Poultney Road offered. From the outside, it had a small front garden with a crooked little path leading to the front door. The windows were finished with hanging baskets that Yvonne had bought along to 'brighten the place up,' but to be honest it did not need brightening. Inside was a hallway where the men had put a tall G-Plan dresser in that, no doubt, would be hung with cups and decorated with no end of cat shaped ornaments. At the end of the hall was a small interior porch leading to a quaint, south facing garden. The lounge was already taking shape with sofas and ornamental display cabinets and the bright little kitchen was full of Poole Potts and other retro pieces.

Steph left the abundance of people downstairs—two removal men, her parents, sister, aunt and uncle—and had taken herself upstairs where there were three small bedrooms. The bathroom was downstairs, which bothered Steph as she was worried that her Nan might need the toilet in the middle of the night and would have a flight of stairs to contend with in the dark. She washed the thoughts from her mind and reconciled them with the beautiful countryside views that surrounded the house. She moved into the smallest room which overlooked the garden. It was only big enough for a single bed and a small wardrobe which had already been granted their place within it. Steph aimlessly sprayed the polish across the wardrobe doors, walking over towards the window sill which she could see needed some of her attention. As she pressed down the nozzle, she listened to the hissing noise that the spray-can made, covering the white finished wood with a fine mist.

Something outside caught her attention. It was at the back of the garden, she could see the hedge moving, as if it were alive. She put down the can and leant further towards the window. There it was again but this time it came out of the hedge and into view. A shaggy dog pushed its way out of the bush and into the sunlight. It had long, dark fur and pointed ears and was so big that Steph wondered how it had made its way into the garden without anyone noticing. She ran as fast as her little legs would take her, throwing her feet one in front of the other, jumping the last three stairs. She pushed into the small glass door of the porch, making it to the back door when something on the wall caught her attention. It was a painting of a large, black and brown dog; one that looked identical to the one she had just seen in the garden. *I didn't know Nanny had a dog,* she thought to herself. She stood on a stool which had been pushed to the side of the long room, and unhooked the photo from the wall.

She tried to open the back door but it was locked so she walked back out into the hall, passing her Uncle Robert as she did.

146

"Are you OK, Steph?" He asked but she did not answer. Instead she just carried on her mission into the lounge where she could get a better look of the garden. Her eyes rummaged through the plants and bushes, the sun still beaming down making the colourful garden look prettier than it probably was. However there was no sign of any animals, let alone a large dog.

She walked back into the hall and out into the front garden where her uncle was standing, looking about the street. There were about fifteen houses, all three bedroomed, overlooking a small green where all the neighbourhood children would play. She thought of how much her Nan would love to watch them. She had always been so good with children.

"Uncle," Steph asked, surprising Robert who seemed to have been lost in thought, "whose dog is this?"

Steph held up the painting, "That's Prince," Robert said, kneeling in front of his niece and taking the large painting from her, "I just put this up. He was the first dog that I ever knew. Such a gorgeous Alsatian – looks ferocious but wouldn't hurt a fly. Why do you ask?"

Steph looked away from her uncle, not wanting him to read her thoughts, "No reason, I just never knew that Nanny had a dog, I knew she loved cats but that's it. Thanks Uncle." She pressed down on to her tiptoes, reaching up and kissed his cheek before running off back inside the house.

She ran through into the kitchen where her Mum was helping Ellen put all of her tinned food away, "Mum, can I have the back door key please?"

"Have you finished with polishing already? It didn't take you long to get bored of the house work did it," Yvonne said, grinning as she took the key from her back pocket. "See if you can find any weeds for me."

Steph took the keys, ran through the house and let herself into the garden. It was empty. She looked about but there was nothing to see. She walked over to the last bush, the one where she had seen the dog, but it was empty. She turned and leant her back against the fence, looking up at the house. She liked how the house was warm and as pretty as you might imagine a cottage from a fairy tale to look. As she was looking up at the house, her sight was drawn to the room where she had just been standing, a small rectangular window directly above the back door. Although the sun was throwing its rays onto the house, she saw movement at the window. *Probably Dad or one of the removal men,* she told herself as she moved into the middle of the garden, still looking up at the window. She saw it again, like a flash of darkness in the sunlight. This time the figure stayed there, looking down in the garden as she had been just moments before. She squinted up, trying to see whether she could recognise the person but as the sun met a cloud in the open sky, she saw the image more clearly. It was not anyone she knew, no one she recognised. *It must be an intruder* she thought, *or one of her neighbours helping with the move,* she tried to reassure herself. She focused, as her mind was able to comprehend what she was seeing. She noted that the person was not wearing what you may expect them to be on such a warm afternoon. It was a man; Steph could see that much and he was wearing a tall black hat. She could not see his face but a chill filtered through her spine.

Again her feet carried her as fast as they could, the muscles in her legs lifting her through the grass, up the step onto the porch, through the hall and up the stairs until she was back on the landing. The landing split both left and right – right to the master bedroom and left to the two smaller rooms over-looking the back of the house. The door to the smaller bedroom was now closed although she knew full well that she had left it open. She walked slowly towards the door, and rested her ear upon it but there was nothing but silence. She pushed against the door but something was blocking it on the other side. She tried pushing harder but still, it did not move.

Floorboards creaked. Steph shuddered, holding her breath to listen. She could hear slow, deep breathing coming from inside the room.

"Hello?" She called out. Nothing. She held her breath again as the creaking floorboards sounded closer to the door on the other side.

The breathing that she could hear receded as Steph was listening to someone inside her nan's new home, laughing. The only laugh that Steph had ever heard that made her want to cry.

Chapter seventeen. Congratulations.

That night Steph was quieter than usual, her parents noticed, mainly Yvonne who was used to her silly humour and active personality but she put it down to the long day they had helping Ellen move.

"Casserole for tea," Yvonne called up the stairs after both Steph and Eric who had both gone up to freshen up, "it's been in the slow cooker all day so it won't take long."

Yvonne busied herself in the kitchen, getting plates and cutlery ready for them around the table, knowing only too well that Eric would more than likely take his dinner in the lounge on his lap. He had never been one for family dining, a TV meal was more his thing, 'who do we want to impress?' He would always say and Yvonne had to agree. Whilst she was taking the mustard from the fridge and pouring Eric a large glass of red wine, she had no idea of the torment that ambushed her nine year old daughters mind.

Steph had taken herself into her bedroom closing the door behind her. She pulled out her pyjamas from beneath her pillow and sat herself on the edge of her bed. Her thoughts were full of still images like photos on a canvas, there for the longevity; she could not forget what her eyes had already seen. There had been someone in her Nan's house that day, someone who came uninvited – but who? She thought of the dog that had distracted her that she had followed outside into the garden. The same dog that had pride of place on Nanny Ellen's wall. Prince or so Uncle Robert had told her. She thought about how it was then that she saw a man dressed in black stood looking at her from an upstairs window, down on the rest of the house. Who was he? Where had he come from?

"Steph! Eric! Dinner's ready!" she heard her Mum calling from downstairs, as she fumbled her way into her bedclothes before running downstairs to join her parents.

She sat watching the episode of *Only Fools and Horses* where Del Boy buys a satellite dish that attracts aeroplanes to his flat. It was funny and took her mind off of the day's events for a little while at least. It was almost ten o'clock before Steph kissed her parents goodnight and took herself upstairs to brush her teeth.

"I'll be up in five minutes," Yvonne called from the kitchen. It seemed that she spent most of her time there, if not cooking then washing up, ironing or some other monotonous chore.

It did not take Steph five minutes before she was tucked up in bed. She had grown out of bedtime stories when she was very little. She had come to enjoy the way characters from her stories sounded in her own mind more than when someone read them to her aloud. Jane used to enjoy reading to her little sister but she was out most nights when Steph was put to bed, She was twenty-two and as independent as anyone else that age, coming and going as she pleased, it was sometimes more like having a lodger than a sister.

Steph was not certain for how long she had drifted into sleep, but she was woken up to raised voices coming from her parent's bedroom and not long after, the front door downstairs slammed. She stood up and listened at her bedroom door, pushing it ajar so that she could hear what her parents were saying.

"She hardly knows him," Yvonne said, Steph sensed the anger in her mother's voice, "it's ridiculous, where are they going to live?"

"They'll sort something, Jane's so independent that she would probably want to move out anyway." Eric replied, almost in Jane's defense.

Is she pregnant? Steph giggled at the prospect of having a nephew when she was only nine herself. *Aunty Steph,* she hid her mouth behind her hand so that her parents would not hear her amusement. She slowly pushed the door open, not ever keeping secrets from her parents, she did not like the idea of eaves dropping on their conversation, she would sooner be a part of it. Making herself known, she walked into her parent's bedroom. The lights were on bright and the duvet was messed in a heap, Jane must have woken them up. *What time is it?* Steph thought, looking about the room for her clock. Five past midnight, she read from the alarm clock next to the bed.

"Steph, go back to bed," Eric asked, looking at his daughter, hoping that she might listen.

"But I can't sleep, what's happening?" She asked, stepping into the room, like she was already a part of the conversation.

"Jane's getting married!" Yvonne exclaimed. She was always the rational one, always the one who calmed a situation but she seemed to be really irate about this. A huge grin plastered itself across Steph's face, and Yvonne could not help but stop for a moment and take some air. *Think logically.*

She had only been twenty when she married Eric and although she knew him for a couple of years first, things were different now. Jane had been seeing Gareth for six months but they had known each other and been in the same circle of friends for some time before that, years in fact.

"You get to be a bridesmaid," Yvonne said, reading Steph's mind as she stood there having still not shifted the smile from her face.

As tears filled Yvonne's eyes, Steph ran across the room and threw her arms around her Mum's neck, "Is Jane still outside with Gareth?" She asked, looking at Eric who did not want to say anything that may aggravate his wife's sudden change of heart. "Get them both inside; we've got some celebrating to do."

It was after one o'clock in the morning that Steph finally returned to bed. She was full of excitement after discussing bridesmaids dresses and hair do's with Jane; her mind was juggling frilly dresses, shoes and dancing. Steph was not overly impressed with the idea of lace and bouquets but the thought of walking down the aisle with her big sister filled her with enthusiasm.

She laid in bed, listening to her parents retire to their bed and Jane wishing goodnight to her fiancé. The house returned to its previous, tranquil state. It was then that she heard it. At first it came as a kind of tapping sound, like water slowly dripping from a tap into a large tin sink. She lay listening, thinking at first that it had started raining outside, sometimes the water dripped from the guttering that obviously needed fixing. As she laid there in the darkness, she felt a chill come over her. She tried pulling herself further under the duvet covering her bed, but the cool air seemed to follow her beneath the covers.

Her teeth chattered, as she lay, peering over the top of the duvet listening to the consistent tap, tap, tapping that was coming from outside her bedroom window. Her eyelids became heavy once again, as she dozed into a peaceful bliss, unaware of the shadow that had walked along the side of her bed. If she had a normal single bed and not one which had her raised six foot above wardrobes and desks, she may have felt her presence but she was now a million miles away, deep within a dream.

She dreamt of a little boy, lost in a field, an open field full of green trees with tiny white daisies cascading the edges. The boy was calling out for his friend, Harry – calling his name over and over. The little boy began to cry, dropping down onto his knees. The sky was full of clouds that gathered above him, casting a shadow beside him, a shadow that he mistakenly took to be his friend. "Harry!" He cried but as he moved, so did the shadow boy sitting next to him. From behind, he could suddenly hear the

154

sound of footsteps running up close and all around him. The soft patting of them against the tall grass that enveloped him as he sat crying by himself. All the while Steph tried to make out his face, but she could not see who this small boy was. Her attention switched to the footsteps. No, not footsteps, they sounded like an animal, quick and light. She could then hear it panting, breathing close by. She looked away from the boy for a moment, who was entirely oblivious to her being there watching him. She saw a dog, Prince, running circles around them. *Prince,* Steph tried to say, trying to settle the animal that was restless and agitated by the lack of attention he was getting. Why was the little boy not looking at him? Why was he not interested in the animal that was so eager for his attention? Steph looked again at the boy who was now standing a small way from Steph, Prince running over to him yet again. The boy was looking at something in the distance, amongst the trees and the bushes, the clouds opened, releasing a shower of rain over the picturesque scene, bringing with it darkness and thunder too. The sky now only lit when the lightning struck. Steph looked onto where the small boy had his attention.

"It was him," the small boy said, straightening out his arm in front of him and pointing into the distance, "it was the man in black." The boy said as he turned to face Steph, "He wants Ellen!"

The boy's scream was what woke Steph. She sat up in her bed, sweating so heavily, her pillow was damp. She turned it over so that she could rest her head on the cold side. It felt nice against her clammy skin. She laid there for a moment or two, the room was silent, and the tapping too had stopped, which she was pleased about as it was one of those annoying noises that aggravated the hell out of anyone trying to fall asleep.

"Steph," it was a distant whisper that she heard coming from the landing.

It was quiet enough that Steph could not recognise the voice, but not quiet enough for her to question whether or not she heard it at all. She sat up listening.

"Steph, come here," the whisper was somehow eager, enticing Steph to follow it. It was soft, a gentle voice that did not make Steph feel threatened in the slightest, but now that she heard it again she knew that it was neither her Mum nor sister. It sounded like a child, not too much older than what she was.

She climbed down the ladder, quietly standing onto the soft carpet that wedged its way through her toes—she wiggled them slightly to make sure that she was in fact awake and not dreaming. Her bedroom door was on ajar, she never liked sleeping with it closed completely. The house was in darkness. Sometimes Yvonne left the bathroom light on, but not that night. She peered through the small opening of the door into the hallway. She could not see anything or anyone.

"Steph," came the voice again, "I need your help." The voice was meek, comforting to young ears. Steph was eager to know who it was that was calling out to her but at the same time, scared to know how, whoever it was, had got inside the house.

As Steph pushed into the door, she thought back to the events that had occurred throughout her life, the unexplainable ones that always left her feeling confused and questioning her own sanity. Had they always been figments of her well-equipped imagination, or was there something else, something completely unexplainable happening to her? She had not ever told her parents about the things she had seen and heard, she did not want them to doubt her. She could run into her parents room and tell them what was happening, but more than likely whatever it was would be gone by the time they got up and they would only see an empty house with no-one but Steph to blame.

She took a deep breath, not sure what it was that she was about to see, and pushed open the door. Although all of the lights in the house were off, there was a gentle glow filling the landing, filtering through from the bedroom at the back of the house. It was as though she was still in a dream-like state, time seemed to stand still, everything around her moving slowly.

Then she saw her. The little girl who was no older than nine years old, long dark hair that fell over her shoulders. She wore a blue and white dress that was complemented by an apron and a matching bonnet. The little girls face was beautiful, happy, a constant smile on her lips.

"Stephanie, come with me, I need your help," the small girl said, never speaking louder than a whisper.

Steph was pulled from her trance-like state, eyes and limbs heavy, by the sound of something moving behind her. Listening, she was certain that it was a teddy that she had not played with for at least a year; her talking Teddy Ruxpin. She turned to face the corner of the room, where she could hear it chattering on about butterflies and sunshine, and slowly walked towards the closed toy box at the back of her bedroom—forgetting all about the little girl waiting for her in the hall.

The toy box was closed. It had a small clasp on the front of it, which she unhooked and released, opening the lid, the bear still playing its tape. She took it out and tried to press the stop button hiding beneath its clothes, but to her surprise, it was not pressed in. She flipped the bear over, moving faster now, and pulled at the battery cover, it was empty but the bear was still talking. She dropped it, pinched herself, to check that there was no chance that she was dreaming. *Ouch!* She thought. She was awake, she knew that much. *The little girl!* Holding the bear by its paw and dragging it along with her, she rushed to the landing. The door at the end of the hall was closed as was her parents and Jane's. She looked down at the bear, which was still rambling, and carried it downstairs, out through the house and into the garden. She tossed it into the dustbin and closed the lid down on top of it.

*****

The next ten months flew by and revolved mainly around the preparations for Jane's wedding which involved sequins, flowers and garters. Yvonne was sticking sequins to almost anything she could get her hands on to embellish the tables, whilst Jane occupied herself trying to find a dress for Steph that was as similar to her own as possible. The day itself was lovely, it was a September wedding and the sun was shining. Jane was a beautiful bride, and Yvonne and Eric made sure that there was nothing that she did not have.

Jane and Gareth enjoyed their honeymoon in Florida and soon returned home to their two bed, semi-detached house in Stansted, Essex. Jane had inherited money after the loss of Mervyn and she invested it wisely. It was only five months before she approached her parents once again with more life-changing news.

"I'm pregnant!" Jane exclaimed. She had never been the maternal type, she had loved it when Steph was young but had never gone out of her way to change nappies or clean up sick, so it was a surprise to everyone; herself included.

Yvonne and Eric were thrilled at the prospect of becoming grandparents. The birth was like many, rather punishing at the time but the rewards soon outweighed the pain and stresses, the nightmares of childbirth were soon forgotten. Jane had a gorgeous little baby boy who they named Jacob. He was welcomed with open arms by everyone. Yvonne had been at the birth and held Jane's hand throughout the very long ten hours.

"She's going to have it tonight," Steph had kept saying, nagging her parents all day, "I get to be an Auntie today," her tone full of anticipation and excitement. An Auntie at just ten years old made her the envy of all her friends.

It was not long after Steph got home from school that Yvonne got the call from Gareth, "We're at the hospital, Jane's in labour," his voice sounding somewhat terrified.

"I'll be right there," and with that, Yvonne grabbed her bag, kissed both Eric and Steph goodbye and was out the door.

Of course, Steph could not sleep, so she had put *The Little Mermaid* on repeat on VHS which took her through until two o'clock in the morning which was when Eric got the call from the hospital. As soon as visitors were allowed, they went up the hospital to meet Jacob. Jane was in her own room, possibly because she had a bad time during labour, but it made their experience in the hospital slightly more bearable. Usually hospitals have that awful smell that can bring back a thousand bad memories to haunt you throughout your life, but that day there were not any smells, just the sound of tiny babies with big, or at least loud, lungs screaming their way through the corridors.

As soon as Steph saw Jane holding Jacob, she ran across the room to her sister who had both Gareth and Yvonne close to her bedside. Jane looked as though she had only just survived a great war with her sweat-coated hair pulled back into a ponytail and her skin quite pale and blotchy, but nonetheless she looked so proud to be holding her son.

"You want a hold?" She asked Steph who was watching Jacob's every move.

"Really? I'd love to," she replied probably louder and much more enthusiastic than she intended which made everyone around her chuckle.

She sat down whilst Jane handed her the huge white blanket that Yvonne had spent weeks knitting, doused in bows and motifs , nothing like the synthetic type that were available to buy on the high street. Somewhere, hidden inside, she met Jacob. She pulled around the edges of the blanket that was enveloping his tiny face, and she felt a tear well in her eye. A feeling like nothing she had ever felt before, so proud of her big sister and so thrilled to be an auntie to such a gorgeous little boy.

Chapter eighteen. Tell no-one.

The bond between the two was instant. Their relationship was more like brother and sister, than aunt and nephew. With just ten years between their ages and Steph not quite grown out of dolls and make believe, Jacob – who had inherited the shortened nickname of Jake, was like one of her dolls only his shit smelt a whole lot worse.

Jane, being the independent woman that she was, wanted to get back to work as soon as she could. Working for her father made the situation easier, being on call should Yvonne need her for anything. Yvonne had taken on the responsibility of looking after Jake during the week whilst both Jane and Gareth worked full-time. Gareth also worked for Eric but unlike Jane who worked in the office, Gareth managed production, so the situation worked fine for the time being.

Steph started secondary school in September 1995 when Jake was about eighteen months old. Yvonne would drop Steph at school and get home in time for Jane to drop Jake off on her way to work. At three-thirty, Yvonne collected Steph from school with Jake and then the two would play for the rest of the afternoon. Seeing him every day, offering to change dirty nappies and feed him, Steph helped teach Jake how to walk among other more mischievous things like climbing stairs and shouting out words in public like 'bottom' and finding it utterly hilarious seeing him get in trouble with Yvonne or Jane. He did pretty much anything Steph encouraged him to do and she loved it.

One Friday evening, Yvonne and Eric had invited Jane and Gareth over for dinner. It was not unusual because Jake was already over and it saved them from cooking when they got home. They ordered an Indian takeaway from the local curry house, the food was pretty consistent and who doesn't love a curry?

When they had all finished their plates, Yvonne cleared away and Jane made the coffees. Steph asked if she could call her friend, Lucy. Lucy was a very pretty little girl with dark brown eyes and long blonde hair that was pinched in tiny ringlets. She had known her since nursery and as Lucy only lived two roads down from Greenmay Close, they would often play together.

"Of course you can, but don't be too long, we've got some profiteroles for dessert," Yvonne said as Steph made her way out to use the phone in the kitchen.

No matter what they ate for dinner, there would always be room for dessert in the Camp household.

Steph dialed the number she had rang a thousand times and Pam answered the phone,
"Hello Steph," she said in her cheery tone, "you want to speak to Lucy?"

"Yes please, is she in?"

"She is," Pam replied, "I'll just call her for you." Steph heard her drop the receiver and shout out her name in the background.

Steph was wearing a strappy dress that she had thrown on after school. It had half a pot of mango chutney thrown down the front of it but was all that she had needed on that hot July evening. The house had remained humid; the windows were open even though there was not a breeze outside. Still, Stephanie suddenly found herself rubbing her arms vigorously against the chill that had slowly spread through them. Steph wished that she had taken the call upstairs so that she could run for a cardigan. Her thoughts were broken when she heard the familiar sound of her friend's voice.

"Hi Steph," she said cheerily through the receiver, "sorry about that, I was just watching the end of Eastenders. Did you know that Sam Mitchell is coming back and it's still going to be that Daniella Westbrook who plays her?"

162

Lucy spoke so fluently that Steph almost lost what she was talking about, "Mum'll be interested, she loves a bit of soap gossip," she said laughing.

"Well she must have more taste than you then," Lucy giggled.

Everyone else was still in the lounge – watching the end of Eastenders no doubt - just a short walk down the hall from where Steph was sitting on the dining room floor. The granite tiles on the floor felt cool against her skin although now she was almost entirely covered in goose pimples. Whilst she chit-chatted with her friend on the phone and what outfit they would wear next to the Coconut Club in Bishop's Stortford, she heard Jake start crying. She could not help but feel like she should go see him, he sounded really distressed. She tried to push aside her youthful, maternal instinct and continued talking to her friend.

"Steph," she heard her sister call from the other room, "he's coming to find you!" Almost instantly, Jake was in the dining room besides Steph, eyes streaming with tears, his skin hot and clammy, "it's OK," she whispered, "calm down you wally."

As she looked down at his face, locked onto his eyes, she saw that there was something other than frustration or annoyance hiding within them. Within the blueness of his baby-eyes, she saw fear. No sooner than she recognised the sign, did her family pet, Holly, come bouncing into the room, skidding across the floor and hiding behind the curtains that were pulled, covering the front of the house.

"You're popular tonight," she heard her Mum and sister teasing in the background whilst her friend continued waffling into her ear about the latest boy she fancied, "Hold on a second Lucy, I…"

Before she had time to finish the sentence, the whole house fell silent, like a spell had been cast upon it. The air around her was not just cold, it was freezing and a small breeze carried itself through the room. Instantly the small

163

hairs on the back of her neck lifted and a shiver raced through her spine. Jake clung tighter round her waist. Holly pushed her nose beneath the drop of the curtain, a quiet growling at the back of her throat as she stared at the door. Steph followed the small dog's gaze and as she watched the empty doorway, she saw, as clear you see any other living person, a woman—tall and wafer-thin, pass by the room where Steph was sitting, now cradling her nephews head, facing the opposite direction—luckily. The woman, who was dressed in a very long, floating white gown, appeared to be gliding through the air. There was no bounce, no hesitation, just a smooth transition from the lounge and along the hall to the bottom of the stairs.

As she passed by the dining room, her head turned. From facing forwards, she shifted to look at Steph, the movement fast, swift as though someone had hit the fast-forward button on the scene. Although Steph never took her eyes from the projection of whatever it was in front of her, she found it hard to establish any features. She had eyes but it was as though they had been frozen open, the pupils were too dilated to see. Her nose was small and her lips thin and pressed tightly together. She appeared to slow down slightly as she passed Steph, as though she was assessing what to do and where to go but she did not stop, just continued to move forwards, on a journey that looked too familiar to interrupt. Steph watched her move to the bottom of the stairs, where she paused momentarily, turning her head away from Steph's frightful stare to look up the stairs, where her body soon followed.

The silence diminished as she could hear her mother calling out to her, like a radio being switched on in a car full of silence, "Steph? Steph? Is everything OK?"

She had not realised that Jake had been screaming, Holly barking. She had dropped the receiver end of the phone on the floor and she could hear the faint sound of a beeping tone, no doubt Lucy would have given up trying to get her

164

attention after the first ten or so seconds. Jane came running into the room, just as Jake stopped screaming, his arm locked around Steph's neck. As Jane began to take him from her, so he began to cry harder.

"It's OK," Steph said, getting to her feet, "I'll bring him back in."

Jane kissed Jake's forehead and made her way back into the lounge, after topping up her cup with another coffee. Steph stepped into the hall, and looked to her left where she had just seen the woman disappear up the stairs. *What if she's waiting for me up there,* she thought, *what if she needs my help?* Steph did not follow her sister's footsteps; she started walking to her left, the opposite direction of the lounge. There were not any lights on at the bottom of the stairs or upstairs, so it was very dark. She looked up them but could not see anything so she flicked the light switch on the wall. It was bright, brighter than the warm glow of the lamp that had been on in the dining room. The landing upstairs was empty, Jake was looking up there too. "It's empty isn't it boy," she said, wiping his damp hair from his forehead, "you really did get yourself in a state didn't you," she said, assessing his tear filled eyes.

At least I know I didn't imagine it, she thought to herself, *but means poor Jake has these eyes too.*

In the dining room, she could hear the phone ringing again, but she was not in the mood to talk about boys right now, she was not in the mood to talk about anything.

Chapter nineteen. A secret shared.

Steph did not speak to Lucy again that night, she asked for her Mum to tell her she come over feeling unwell and had gone to bed. Yvonne probably thought that they had an argument. Lucy probably thought the same about Steph and her parents, although it would have been unusual due to their close relationship. But neither one of them questioned it.

Steph knew that she would tell Lucy what was going on in her life but not until she had figured it out herself. She wanted to wait until they were alone at school the next day. She knew that the time had also come that she would probably tell her Mum too. A few things had happened to her that she had wanted to share with Yvonne but was too confused herself to be able to rationalise enough to share with anyone, even her parents. She decided that she would open up to Lucy and see what she thought about it before she told anyone else. For years she had managed to conceal it, but it seemed that now Jake was involved too, she did not want to encourage him to keep things bottled up.

Going to an all-girls school had both positive and negative implements on a young girl's life. You either grew into a very close knit of girls, or you didn't. Steph did, for a few years anyway. She got herself in with the popular group – popular with teachers, with other girls and with boys. The two girls clicked on the first day at the school and were instantly inseperable. The school itself had been voted in the top fifty schools in the country for several years running. Steph was out of the catchment area but because her sister had been a pupil eight years earlier, she was accepted. Her tom-boyish behaviour and dress sense was soon replaced by nail varnish, lip gloss and mini-skirts. The change-over was subtle and as well as being expected, was a pleasant change from wanting to climb trees and dress the same as her friends of the opposite sex. Boy friends had always remained in Steph's life but when her friend Andrew had moved away three years earlier, it felt as though she had lost a major part of her adolescence and encouraged her to grow up. This was possibly why she dealt with things so maturely, why she did not go crying to her parents at any given opportunity and why she sometimes felt as though she carried the weight of the world on her shoulders; because she knew that sometimes, it was the best thing to do.

It was raining that Monday morning so at lunchtime, Steph had asked Lucy to meet her in their form room. It would probably be busy but it was dry.

"Oh dear God, I hate history," Lucy whined as she walked into the room, "Mr Briggins likeness to Tom Hanks is the only thing that keeps me awake for the hour I'm in there," she said. Steph giggled as she had never seen the similarity. "What is it you wanted to talk to me about anyway? Is everything OK? Your Mum said you weren't well last night."

"I was fine," Steph replied, "well my health was fine anyway. Look Lucy I need to tell you something and I don't want you to look at me like I'm crazy, I just want someone else's opinion on something."

"OK." Lucy said, pulling her chair in closer to her friend and pushing her bag down on the floor beneath the desk, "you have my attention, don't leave me hanging!"

Two girls, Jessica and Julie had been sat at the front of the room revising for a math exam they had, but both stood up and made their way out of the door and into the corridor outside. Steph started from the night she had watched *A Nightmare on Elm Street,* about how she had been woken by a nightmare that had continued long after she was awake. She told her about the small girl she had seen in her house, the man in black who had been at her Nan's house and finally she got to the real reason she had not wanted to

168

carry on with their phone call the night before. Of course she had no memory of the supernatural occurrences that followed her when she was a child.

Lucy did not say anything. In fact she did not say a word the whole time Steph was speaking—which was unlike Lucy who would usually have something to say about everything. She just sat completely motionless, looking at Steph, watching her every move.

"Are you being completely serious?" Lucy said, finally.

"I swear," Steph said, pushing herself back into her chair, huffing out of breath heavily, like a sigh of relief.

"It isn't that I don't believe you; of course I do, it's just difficult to imagine. So basically, what you're telling me is that you see ghosts?"

Steph sat still, it was the first time anyone had said the word *ghost* and now that it had been thrown out there, it sounded silly.

"I guess so," Steph answered, quietly, squinting her eyes, looking about the room, taking in the notion, "Yeh, that is what I'm saying."

Neither one of the girls spoke as the door to the form room opened and a girl named Hayley, which neither one of them knew too well, walked in, smiled over at them and took a seat at the front of the class. Before they could say anything else, the bell rang; lunch was over.

"Come over mine tonight, after dinner, about seven o'clock," Lucy said, as she bent down, lifted her bag on to her lap and pulled out a pen and paper for the class, "I've got something I want to show you."

*****

Although Steph only lived a five minute walk from Lucy, Yvonne did not want her walking there alone. There were too many horror stories on the news and too many missing people ads in the paper, so she offered to drive her

169

round after clearing away after dinner. It was still light outside, the sun did not fall from the sky until shortly before bedtime, so there was plenty of time left to see whatever it was that Lucy wanted to show her. It had bugged her all afternoon, Steph was not able to concentrate on any of her classes or any of what her teachers were rambling on about. She hated being left in the dark about anything, especially something that had her so curious.

She helped her Mum clear away, throwing all of the plates and cutlery into the dishwasher as fast as she could. "Blimey Steph," Yvonne said as she wiped the gravy that had spilt on the kitchen top, "what's keeping you? I've never seen you this eager to get out."

"Lucy's got a surprise for me, I'm excited, that's all."

"Sounds ominous," Yvonne said, grinning, "leave that," she said, looking at the dirty dishes she still had balancing in her hands, "you go wait in the car, I just have to pop to the loo."

By the time Steph had grabbed a cardigan to pull over her tight, cropped top and baggy combat-style trousers, Yvonne met her out at her car and within just a few minutes, she was sitting outside twenty-four Fairview Drive.

"Thanks Mum, I'll get Pamela to drop me home later, I don't think I'll be long."

"Just make sure you're home before nine o'clock, "Yvonne said, reciprocating the kiss her daughter planted on her cheek.

Before Steph made it all the way up the front garden path, the front door opened and little Lucy was stood in the doorway, "I thought you'd chickened out," she said, grabbing a set of house keys from the bottom step, "we may as well go straight out, no doubt you have to be home before sundown."

Steph nudged her elbow into her friend's arm. She was always being teased about her parents being strict. It did not

170

really bother her, she liked how much her mother cared but it aggravated her that her friends tried to wind her up about it. She had learnt that the best way to react was not to react but sometimes she could not help it.

"Where are we going anyway," Steph asked, pulling her arms into her cardigan, "what is it you wanted to show me? It's been bugging me all day."

"OK…" Lucy began, "so there's this house, about ten minutes' walk from here. It's huge and has been vacant for years. I think someone may have bought it now because they've taken all of the old windows out and have started to replace them. But there are some that haven't been replaced yet and just have sheets hanging over them,"

"And…"

"And, we can get in and take a look inside." Lucy said, excited.

"What for?" Steph had always loved an adventure, had always been intrigued by the unknown but when the unknown had become the kind of haunting that you had no power over, it all became a little less inviting. "I'm not sure."

"Are you kidding me! Were you talking crap earlier then about having some kind of psychic ability?"

"I'm not psychic!" Steph said, holding back a smile that was forcing its way onto her lips, "I've just seen stuff, that's all."

"Well I haven't seen that sort of 'stuff' so it must be some sort of supernatural link that you have with the dead." Steph actually laughed aloud this time. "You can laugh but none of my other friends have seen ghosts walking around their homes and their families homes come to think of it. Come on, it'll be interesting and if it's not, it'll be fun at least. If you do have some sort of psychic power, then going to a place like this will prove it. I've heard that it's super haunted, loads of people around Sawbridgeworth have done Ouija boards there and they've actually worked."

Steph walked alongside her friend, thinking. She liked the idea, she was always up for anything but she was worried that whatever it was that was following her would find her there, "I don't want to put you in any danger," Steph said, slowing down.

"I'm a big girl, I can handle it. And anyway, I love this kind of stuff."

The girls walked through a large open park at the back of Lucy's house that was surrounded by trees and lush greenery. They followed a small gravel footpath that lead to a track off of the marked path, "it's up there," Lucy said, knocking a spider from her brow that must have fallen from one of the trees, "you ready?"

"Course I am," Steph said as the girls started on their way up a very long, narrow path fit only for a small car.

It was not long before the house came into view. It was huge with three storeys and four windows on every level on the front of the house. Lucy had been right, all of the windows were either boarded up or covered with a sheet that hung from the top. If the wind had been blowing, they would have been blowing in its direction but the night was still and so was the house. It was built of red brick and a large wooden front door. It must have been set on several acres of land, although it was hard to tell with a brick wall surrounding the house.

"Are you sure we won't get in trouble for this? How do you know the police haven't put traps in place to catch people like us?" Steph asked, slowing down her pace as they approached the largest window downstairs.

Lucy laughed, "Don't be silly, I've been here before and look," she pulled on the board that concealed the missing glass, "we don't even have to break in, someone's already done it for us."

Both girls squeezed their way through the small gap that emerged as they pulled the corner of the board from the empty frame. Lucy went in first and Steph followed close behind, trapping her leg between the wood and the brick, "Damn!" she cursed, pulling her leg through and losing a sheet of skin with it, baring a damp redness that stung as the air hit it.

She jumped down a little less awkwardly and met her friend inside. Having a good look about, she saw that they had landed themselves in what looked to be the lounge. There was an old, inglenook fireplace and a small, leather two-seater sofa next to it. Steph could see that the wallpaper had more than likely, once been vibrant and colourfully decorated with flowers, but now it looked worn and dull. Curtain poles remained above the empty windows and the floorboards looked damp in places where the rain had made its way through the glassless frames. Steph crept across the floorboards which still creaked and whined beneath her tiny frame. Lucy stayed put.

"Come on," Steph said eagerly, "you're the one who wanted to come here. Don't chicken out now!"

Reluctantly, Lucy made her way across the room, following in Steph's shadow, had she had one, over to the door. Steph, with not an iota of fear, reached out to the door knob and turned it. The catch jumped and the door slipped open, Steph let go of the knob and let the door reveal the huge, open plan hallway in front of them.

"Wow!" Lucy said, stepping forwards, through the door and onto the tiled floor of the hall, "this place is creepy."

Steph's eyes squinted slightly, "I thought you said you'd been here before?" She then knew for sure that Lucy had lied. She was silly to have thought that Lucy would have had the nerve to trespass somewhere like that by herself.

As she looked about she saw the large, brightly-coloured graffiti that covered the walls and the cobwebs that floated from the coving in the corners of the room like candy floss around a spinner. Whilst Steph crept through the open room, she passed a large, curved staircase to her right. She would admit that the place was unnerving, like something straight from a horror movie, but at the time she did not feel any sort of connection; nothing that drew her further into the house.

She stopped walking, "What is it?" Lucy asked, taking a slow step back, "Do you hear something?"

Steph smiled to herself. She could really play a game with this one, "Yeh, didn't you hear that?" She said, pointing to the door ahead of them, "it sounded like footsteps." Steph knew full well there was no one or nothing else inside the huge derelict manor house besides them, the place had been empty and deserted for years, but all the same, the opportunity to wind up her friend was too tempting.

Lucy turned away from Steph and slowly crept towards the door. If she was being honest, Steph was surprised by Lucy's heroism. Perhaps she was trying to prove that she wasn't as scared as what Steph made her out to be. Steph watched as her friend's little Reebok Classics tiptoed their way across the tiled floor, so eager and full of anticipation at what she may find hiding behind there. In a way, Steph envied her friend who was completely naïve to the afterlife and supernatural occurrences. Her options were broad and her beliefs were just an extension of what her parents had taught her—just how children's minds should be—completely pure.

"Come on," Steph said, "I was just winding you up. Let's go." Steph turned on her heel and started back the way she came, feeling disheartened and tired of the pretence.

"No," Lucy said, "I think you were right. There's someone in there."

Steph turned to face her friend but she was nowhere in sight. She turned her head to examine the room, her breathing becoming a little more forced, "Stop it, Lucy, I'll leave without you."

She sounded strong but inside, her nerves were being tested, "That's it, I'm going," but as she turned around and took her first step forwards, her friend came flying out from behind a huge mahogany dresser.

"BOO!!" She yelled, Steph jumped and almost slapped her friend around the face, but she knew that really she deserved it. Both girls burst into hysterics, holding their stomachs as though they ached with pain.

"Come on, let's get out of here before we get caught."

Both girls retraced their steps and exited the building via the window they had entered whilst talking about the possibilities that could have been and ghosts that Steph did not believe for a second haunted the old brick house. When they had made it outside, the warm breeze returned to blanket their skin.

"It could have been winter being inside that place," Lucy said as she spun round to give the house one last look.

She paused, not moving anything besides her eyes which grew wider as she stared, "Lucy? What is it?"

Steph turned to meet her friends gaze. She looked at the window that they had just climbed through and there was nothing but the wooden barrier, which was a little worn and beaten at the edges but still intact. The front door was still closed and the surroundings were empty. She looked back at Lucy who was lost in the place, her eyes looking up towards the windows of the third floor. Steph turned to see what her friend was so fascinated by and as she did she saw movement. The third floor windows were covered by sheets, long, heavy industrial-looking sheets—the sort that would keep the rain out and put trespassers off of entering. When they arrived an hour or so earlier, the sheets were still to match the wind, which on that summer evening was non-existent. But not anymore, as she watched in awe, they were moving, blowing hard as though there was a gale-force wind attacking it from both sides.

"Impossible," Steph said as her expression became similar to Lucy's, both girls completely transfixed.

As they watched in amazement they noticed that although they knew it was not any kind of wind that was blowing the material, they could see that it was something inside the building that was forcing it to move.

"Do you see what I'm seeing?" Lucy asked as she raised her arm to point at the manifestation of a hand coming through the sheets.

Another hand, and then another, like arms reaching from the pits of hell, struggling for salvation. Within moments, the shapes of hands that were forming in the material were accompanied by several faces stretching through it. They could not see skin or eyes, but just the outline of human faces pushing their way out of the building into the restriction of the sheets that was covering their escape.

"I'm getting out of here!" Lucy yelled, as she turned on her heel and ran back down the winding gravel path to the road which led to her house, back to where she knew she would be safe.

Steph hesitated. Standing alone, she didn't move. She had to make sure that what she was seeing was real, that she was not imagining it. Over the years she had learnt that most things children were frightened of would simply vanish if they closed their eyes and counted to ten. It worked for her most of the time, ninety-nine percent of the time. But then there was that one percent of the time that it failed.

One–two–three–four–five–six–seven–eight–nine-ten, she counted fast in her head. She opened her eyes, and it was still there, still happening. But this time the faces had turned as though they were looking down at her. She did not wait any longer. She did not need to see any more as she turned around and ran. She ran as fast as her skinny little legs would carry her. She did not follow Lucy. She did not want to waste time running down the road to her house.

176

She could call and check on her later. She fled the gravel path, passed the sign that pointed in the direction of Lucy's road and up the hill that led to Greenmay Close. It was then that she stopped running and tried to compose herself. There was no way she could let her mum see her running in such a state, it was going to be bad enough that she had walked home by herself. It was just something else she would have to try not to explain.

Chapter Twenty. Home alone.

The following week flew by. Steph had not seen that much of Lucy as she had taken three days off from school that week complaining of stomach flu. Steph had called her when she got home after their visit to the old house, but Pam had apologised on Lucy's behalf and explained that when she got home, she felt unwell and took herself straight to bed. Yvonne had been pretty annoyed that Steph had not called her for a lift home or that Pam had not offered her one but Steph explained that she was closer to home after their walk than she was to Lucy's house so it made sense to go straight home. Yvonne was just happy that Steph had made it back safely.

When Lucy returned to school that Friday, she had not looked unwell and it seemed that she had spent most of the day trying to avoid Steph. They would usually walk together between lessons but Lucy was nowhere to be found even though Steph had spent most of her free time looking for her. It was obvious she was avoiding her, but why?

Finally, after lunch, they both had to be in the form room for registration. Steph was there first, she had not been hungry and had some math homework to catch up on so she got to class early and saved Lucy a seat. Lucy came into the room by herself and walked sheepishly towards Steph with her head down and her shoulders limp.

"Where the hell have you been?" Steph asked, putting her pen down. "I've been looking everywhere for you and why have you been missing my calls and getting your mum to lie to me, I'm not stupid. What's up with you?"

Lucy pulled her chair in further to the desk, "I'm sorry, I guess I can't handle things as well as you can. The other night really freaked me out. I mean, it did happen didn't it?

I'm not imagining things? There were faces, or something, filling those windows…"

"It sounds crazy but yeah, it happened and we both saw it," Steph said, smiling inwardly that Lucy admitted she saw it too. It was the first time someone else had bared witness to the paranormal activity that had been haunting her for years and at long last she had confirmation that she was not going mad.

As Steph went to continue, she was interrupted by their form tutor, Mrs Lanthorn who graced them all with her ungainly presence, "Come on girls, sit down, we haven't got all day," she said as she wiped her long, side-swept fringe from the perspiration that swamped her forehead. She had never liked Lucy much, "Burton, can you please give me more attention than you're giving Stephanie, I'm sure I have more interesting things to say."

Lucy giggled. Steph took out the pen she had just put away and wrote on the corner of her notepad,
I'm babysitting Jake tonight—get over about 7pm if you're free? Talk then?
Steph looked at Lucy quickly who nodded in her direction. *Typical*, Steph thought as she lost all interest in anything Mrs Lanthorn had to say, *I found her but I can't bloody talk to her!*

*****

Jane and Gareth were taking Yvonne and Eric out for dinner to thank them for looking after Jake whilst they both worked full-time. The gratitude was not always so obvious but Yvonne had been working herself to the bone and even Jane had appreciated her devotion. They were being treated to a Chinese at the Peking Palace in Sawbridgeworth, not far from where they lived.

"Lucy's coming over in a bit, Mum, is that OK?" Steph asked, flicking from *Sister, Sister,* to *Fresh Prince of Bel*

Air. "We're just going to watch TV and play with Jake, she's not seen him for ages."

"No need to explain," Yvonne said, not looking up from the mirror as she finished off her eyes with a coat of mascara, "Jane's meeting us there so she won't even know, but I doubt she would mind. Lucy's like one of the family." Eric did not come in to get changed, he beeped the horn from his car outside on the drive, "We won't be late love, if you need me, you have the restaurant's number."

She kissed Steph on the forehead and Jake on his cheek and made her way out the front door. Steph admired how lovely her mother looked wearing a black a-line skirt and fitted red jacket pinched in at the waist. There was never a time Steph could remember Yvonne not looking immaculate.

It was thirty minutes or so before Lucy came over. Yvonne had already fed Jake and done Steph's dinner so, being a warm evening, Steph went outside to play with Jake. Holly pottered about the garden, squatting in almost every inch of it. Yvonne and Eric had built a wooden Wendy house for Steph when she was seven and it still stood tall at the bottom of the garden, beyond the patio and the lawn but before the huge row of Ash trees that shielded the house from the small stream that ran behind it. It was a cute little house, big enough for a plastic table and chairs, pretend oven and some bean bags. The perfect little hideaway for a game of make believe. Steph had grown out of the den a few years earlier but Jake was only just approaching the age that became interested in such novelties. She watched as Jake grabbed at plastic pots and pans, not quite knowing what they were used for, so he opted to bashing them on everything in sight. He was a cute little boy with similarities of both his parents. The resemblance he had of his mother's eyes made Steph feel as though she was playing with her older sister and not her baby nephew.

In the distance, Steph heard the doorbell chime. Jake barely acknowledged it and continued to make conversation with whomever was a part of his imaginary game whilst he chatted and bashed about his plastic kitchen utensils. Steph checked on Holly who was still pondering which spot of the garden she would mark next and ran quickly into the house to greet Lucy. Kicking off her shoes, she ran through the lounge. It had felt cold compared to the garden that was like a sun trap during the summer months.

"Hey!" Steph jumped as she pulled open the front door. She had been looking forward to seeing her friend and getting to the bottom of why she had been acting so strange.

"Hey," Lucy replied, smiling briefly and looking slightly more comfortable than how she had at school earlier that day. Stepping into the hallway, Lucy looked about, "Is Jake not here?"

"Yeh, he's in the garden playing in the Wendy house. You must remember the fun we used to have in there?" Steph said, saying anything to make Lucy crack a smile.

"Mud cakes right? Yes," she started with a grin, "remember the time I shoved one in your face after you winding me up that I fancied Adam Locks?" She laughed, "That'll teach ya!"

Both girls cracked in fits of laughter. Lucy finally finding her sense of humour. Steph felt as though she had her friend back at last after days fearing that she may have lost her.

They stayed inside for a while, talking about school and boys and the travesty that Lucy was going to have to miss the Coconut Club disco the following weekend as she would be away in Devon with her parents. Deep in conversation, Steph had not noticed Holly scoot across the garden, the lounge and out into the dining room. Soon after, their conversation was interrupted by an almighty thud in the garden and they heard Jacob start screaming. Steph

182

moved first as her heart skipped a beat. The sound of Jake's screams were not that of a child seeking attention, it was more of pain or fear, an uncontrollable cry for help. By the time she reached the patio steps which lead up to the lawn, Jake was already running halfway across it, tears streaming down his red, sweaty face. Steph immediately noticed that he had a small tear in his Postman Pat t-shirt. She caught him in her arms just as his little legs gave in and he collapsed down onto her,

"Caught you!" Steph said, lifting Jake up to her whilst his legs kicked and head shook ferociously, "Jake? Jacob! What's the matter?"

She ran him to the house and passed Lucy who was standing still in the doorframe not really knowing what to do, "What's wrong with him?" She asked, feeling somewhat of a loose part in the situation.

Steph sat with Jake on her lap, stroking his head and calming him, for almost fifteen minutes. She was surprised her neighbour Carol did not come over to see what all the fuss was about. She was a good friend of Yvonne's so it was likely she too, was out with her husband Michael. When Jake had finally stopped crying, Steph was able to speak to him. Unlike most two year olds, Jake was still struggling with his speech as he had an impairment that caused him to not be able to pronounce his words properly, causing him to mix them around and slur a sentence into one long word when he was upset and not concentrating. Therefore Steph had to listen hard to what he was saying.

"What happened, Jake? Did you hurt yourself?" Steph asked, stroking the corner of his sleeve that had the tear in the material.

Jake shook his head.

"Did you panic that I wasn't there?"

Again, he shook his head and his eyes slowly began to fill with tears like a tap was gushing through them. Lucy sat down next to them, and was playing with the shoe lace on

183

Jake's mini Classics when she saw a red mark on his leg. Not wanting to draw attention to it, she nudged Steph's arm and pointed it out without Jake noticing her. It was a ring that stretched around the girth of his ankle. It was bright pink with underlying tones of purple where a bruise was forming.

Steph asked again, this time there was panic hidden within her tones, "Jake what happened in the garden?" She had turned the small child so that she was looking him directly in the eye.

"A man," Jake said, finally, "there was a scawy man. I fink he wanted to hurt me."

Steph sat still when Lucy suddenly got to her feet, "I'm sorry Steph but after Monday, I'm not listening to this shit. Sorry!" She said, throwing her hands over her mouth, apologising for cursing in front of Jake, "I'm going home."

Before Steph had time to react, Lucy had already slammed the front door closed behind her. The aunt and nephew sat motionless for a moment, Jake probably even more frightened now that there was just the two of them and Steph not feeling too far from the same.

"What did the man look like? Did he look like Daddy?" Steph asked finally.

Jake shook his head.

"Come on Jake, tell me what you saw."

"A big black coat," Jake said, looking at the floor. "He shouting at me and hurted me," he blurted out along with a flow of tears that now poured from his eyes. He hid his face in Steph's shoulder, "his face looked like the man on your book."

Steph wondered who he meant. "What book?" She asked.

"I'll show you," Jake said composing himself and jumping from her lap. He led her by her hand through the house and up the stairs to the landing. She had never realised how long the hallway was, that night it felt lengthier than ever. Jake continued to tug at her hand as he led her to the end of the long, narrow landing and into her bedroom at the back of the house. She walked in and looked at Jake, who had dropped her hand whilst his eyes ransacked the room.

Finally he pointed at something on the wall, "That one," he said, a satisfying expression slapped across his face.

Steph walked over to the book case that Jake was pointing at and on the binding of the book he pointed out, out of the fifty or so other books that sat on that shelf, were a pair of dirty yellow coloured eyes peering out through a drain.

"That's not a man," Steph said to her nephew who looked so small and fragile in front of her, "that's just a pretend character in a story and in fact is just his eyes," she explained.

"I could only see his eyes, all his face was hiding under his black hat. He was angry, he told me off and tried to hit me..." Jake looked as though he was going to cry again and Steph felt her own eyes well up but she did not want Jake to see that.

She cuddled him, squeezing him tightly whilst she tried to make sense of the situation. There were only two options. One was that someone had broken into the garden, maybe over the side gate whilst Steph and Lucy were sitting inside. Or, it could somehow, possibly be the same man that she had seen a few years ago at her nan's house on the day she had moved in. He too was dressed in black and wore a distinctive black top hat. She shuddered as she remembered that the back door to the house was left open and that out of either of those two options she had given herself, meant that whatever or whoever it was that Jake had seen, could still be out there, in the garden or worse still, inside the house.

She stood up, sitting Jake down on her new single bed she had gotten a few years before when she had grown out of her cabin bed, and switched on the small television that was on top of her white-finished chest of drawers. "OK, I need you to be a big boy for me," she tried to explain, "I won't be long, I have to check on Holly, then I'll be right back upstairs with you." Jake's lips began to quiver, "It's fine, don't be silly, I won't be long." She left an episode of *Rosie & Jim* on, a cartoon about two rag dolls that cruised about a river on a narrow boat – it was enough to take anyone's mind off of pretty much anything.

Steph left the room, closing the door behind her, hoping that Jake would stay where she left him, safe and out of harm's way. She crept slowly across the landing, passing the room where she had once seen the small girl that had beckoned her, haunting her vision, but now the room was empty. She carried on to the top of the stairs and down them, passing the front door. She looked through into the lounge, the sliding door was still wide open, and she could feel the cool breeze blowing through the house, causing a chill to carry down her spine. She stood in the doorway of the dining room as she heard Holly's soft whimpering coming from within the room. She stepped inside, and looked about,

"Holly? Holly?" She whispered, hoping that the dog would creep out from its hiding place, but the small grey and white Lhasa Apso remained hidden.

Steph walked through the dining room, checking behind the dresser and under the table and then into the kitchen which she could clearly see was empty. The curtains covering the large patio windows at the front of the house were partially pulled together, allowing light to stream through into the room. There was certainly enough room behind them for a small dog to be hiding. As she thought it, she saw the drapes to the right hand side of the window move just a fraction as the cries of the animal continued.

"Holly?"

Steph knelt onto all fours and moved over to where her companion was hiding. She didn't want to startle her as something obviously already had. She reached out to grab the corner of the curtain, to pull it back and reveal the frightened dog and as she did, the sound of the animal's cry grew louder and more scared, like an animal cowering in defence. She counted to three in her mind, *one...two...*but just before she could think...*three*...She heard a dog barking in the garden that sounded like Holly. But if it was Holly in the garden, then what was it behind the curtain?

Part of her hesitated. Her instinct to react was delayed. One part of her questioned whether she really want to know what was eating at her curiosity? What was playing games with her sanity? The other part, the more assertive dimension of her conscious—the same part which followed in her grandfather footsteps—urged her to reach forward, just a fraction as she tugged on the edge of the curtain. Revealing nothing but an empty dog's basket, she caught a glimpse of something, or someone small, running past the dining room door and down the hallway.

She shuffled to her feet, her socks slipping on the polished tiles. She couldn't move quick enough, Jake was alone upstairs with whatever it was that had just joined him up there. She threw herself up the stairs, tripping over the top step and tearing the skin on her knees as she fell across the dry carpet. She paused again, briefly this time, as she listened to her nephew talking to someone in her bedroom; his voice, then theirs; as clear as if she was in the room with them being a part of the conversation. Bursting through the door, she looked straight to the bed where she had left him. He was still there but not sitting down like he had been, he was leaning onto the window sill, looking out of the window into the back garden, his face flushed and anxious.

"That's him!" He cried, "the man, Stepney, it's the man! The little girl just showed me him. She said that she's fwightened of him too." Steph shot across the room and scooped the child up into her arms as her eyes just briefly looked down into the garden. She saw Holly on the lawn, barking wildly across the garden at the Wendy house. She instantly saw him inside the small, wooden playhouse. He was too tall to be inside, but somehow he was hiding behind the small square window next to the tiny red, wooden door. As she looked harder, she saw what Jake had tried to describe earlier by pointing out a cover of one of her horror books but what she was looking at did not resemble anything she had ever seen before. Whatever it was that she was looking at, was the epitome of evil. Without a doubt she knew that he was the enigmatic figure that had been in her Nanny Ellen's new house. The man that she thought now resided in her Nan's spare room, but for whatever reason, was there at Greenmay Close, watching them.

She turned and ran out of the bedroom, through the top of the house and down the stairs. She reached for the door and twisted the key, turning the lock and almost made it outside when she saw Jane's purple Vauxhall Tigra pull around the corner of the road, and her parents' car following close behind. They pulled up outside the house as Steph stepped out into the cool air, enjoying the breeze on her sweat-filled chest and face and sat down on the doorstep.

Yvonne jumped out of the car and came running over to her, "Whatever's the matter?" She asked, bending down to cuddle her daughter.

"I'll tell you later," Steph said, "I want to stay outside for a minute, Mum. I just need to calm myself down. Please can you go and check on Holly though and make sure no one is in the garden, I thought I saw someone."

Yvonne looked at her with alarm and ran straight into the house. Steph knew that no-one would be there, and that the time had now come in which she needed to tell her

188

parents what was going on. She needed to open up to them with what she had been hiding for years. That she believed that something or someone was haunting her.

Twenty-one. The secret's out.

Yvonne searched the garden and then the house. Steph had unnerved her by telling her that she thought she saw someone out there. Their house was secure and there would be no reason for Steph to imagine that someone was there. It was only eight o'clock so the sun was still high and nestled in the sky. Steph knew all too well that she would have no choice but to tell her Mum what had really been going on. She knew that she would not hear the end of it otherwise.

She waited until Jane and Gareth had left with Jake and things had settled down inside the house. She did not want to open up to her mum as the result of being forced into it, she wanted to tell her because she felt that she deserved to know. They left Eric downstairs watching a boxing match on a Sky Sports channel he had paid a fortune for and spent some time getting ready for bed. When Steph was ready she went into her mum's room. They would often watch something together on television before Steph retired to her bedroom so her behaviour was not unusual.

They sat for a while until Steph could not hold it in any longer, "Mum, can I talk to you?"

"Of you course you can," Yvonne replied, "let me turn this down," she said, reaching for the remote. "What's wrong? I could tell that something's on your mind. Is it about what happened earlier today?"

Yvonne sounded so sincere that it made opening up to her a lot easier. Steph started back as far as she could remember. About the night that she had been woken by a young girl calling to her from the back bedroom, about the man in black she had seen at her Nanny Ellen's and that she had seen him again, that night, in their garden and that she thought that Jake had seen him too.

191

"I'm scared that he will hurt Jacob," Steph said, feeling a lump form in the back of her throat, "He had a tear in his t-shirt from playing in there earlier. What if it was the same man that I have been seeing?"

Yvonne had not spoken a word. She let her daughter say all that she had to before she spoke. "Steph, I knew you were special the moment that I held you in my arms, in fact it was before that. I knew the moment I found out I was pregnant with you. Your Granddad Dick made a promise to me before he died. He told me that one day he would come back from the dead as one of my animals as he knew how well I treated them. It was always a bit of a joke we shared but then three months after he had died, I found out I was three months pregnant with you, even though for thirteen years, doctors had told me that I couldn't have any more children."

"Was Granddad religious?" Steph asked, never before asking too many questions about Richard.

"Not really," Yvonne answered, still unsure of how much she would let on about him, "but he had beliefs and he believed that when we die, sometimes, some people come back or just never leave in the first place. If their death was sudden or manipulated; or because their souls are too evil to find peace, they linger in a limbo between our life and the next—wherever that may be."

Steph was engrossed. "But that doesn't explain what I have to do with it, or who the man is that keeps following me."

"Don't you see? The life of your grandfather lives in you, you have so many of his qualities, so many talents that you share. It's unfortunate, but he also carried with him a gift," Yvonne said. Thinking hard about how to phrase what she had to say next to her young daughter made her face crumple, "he had a gift that allowed him to help people." Yvonne stopped speaking for a moment.

192

"What sort of people? Why did they need helping?" Steph asked, more confused than before they first started their chat.

"He helped those people who are trapped, people who need releasing. Who need to find their peace."

"But who is the man in black?" Steph asked again, her voice more stern than before.

"To be honest, I don't know. The best person to ask is Nanny Ellen. She knows a whole lot more about him than I do, but I know that she will warn you not to get too close. He's not kind-hearted and you should not entertain him."

"You want me to ignore him?" Steph asked, recognising the underlying current of caution in her mother's voice.

"As best you can, Steph, but speak to Nanny and see what she says."

*****

Steph went to bed that night with her mind buzzing. Her parents had never opened up to her before about anything like that. She guessed that they had not really needed to. They had never had a reason to tell her anything. Little did Steph know that Yvonne had known about her 'gift' for years, she had just hoped that Steph had not come to realised it herself.

Chapter twenty-two. More than one.

The next day was Saturday and Steph was woken by the sunshine as it crept through her curtains. She felt the weight lifting from her shoulders. As if there had been physical weights holding her down that had finally been taken away. Although it did not really make any difference to her situation, she knew that her mother would always know the right thing to do. Now that she had someone she could confide in who would not run away every time something untoward happened. At least she hoped that she wouldn't.

As she lay in bed, one leg hooked around the side of her duvet she thought back to the night before; about what had occurred before her parents had arrived home. Were there any signs that she had missed? She might not be the seven year old girl who loved to play detective but some degree of inquisitiveness remained in her character. Over the years she had become very aware of her surroundings, and that left her keenly perceptive of what happened around her. Like retracing steps to find a misplaced set of keys, or finding lost property in the most unlikely places. She was also good at sensing the intent of a person. Like knowing if someone's character is good or not. She liked the saying that if an animal does not like someone then neither should you. As she got older, her sixth-sense (which everyone has to some degree), became stronger.

In 1996, Jane was pregnant for a second time. It had been the very early stages of pregnancy but Steph was thrilled at the prospect of being an auntie again. One night, she had a dream that she was out shopping in Harlow with her Mum and Jane when Jane had taken a fall down moving escalators, hitting every sharp step on her way. Steph watched in horror as she saw her sister emerge in a pool of blood, her baby bump sinking down into an abyss. The next morning, she walked into her Mum and told her that she 'knew' Jane would lose the baby and two days later, she did. Of course this could be fate or it could be intuition, but maybe it could also be a psychic ability that some people are born with.

As she got older, the visions, or dreams that showed her things became less frequent but occasionally she still got 'feelings' about certain things.

As she felt herself drifting back into sleep, the doorbell rang downstairs. She remembered that Jane was bringing Jake round so that she could do some shopping. Hopefully Jake would not think too much about what had happened the night before. He was still only young and hopefully, would put it down to his imagination, or however it is that young children envision their imaginary friends – those Jake had plenty of.

She turned herself over in the bed and looked at the clock, it read 10:21. She did not have any plans for the day so decided to stay home with her mum and Jake and maybe pop round to Lucy's later on that day. She could not believe that her friend had left when she did, and did not even phone later during the evening to check that everything was OK. Maybe she wouldn't bother visiting her later on that afternoon after all. Steph would find out the hard way a few years later that a lot of the friendships she made at school were phony.

She got up, dressed and made her way downstairs. Jane had come alone with Jake and was drinking coffee with Yvonne, both black, no sugar. *Yuck*, Steph thought, never understanding what tastes anyone would need to enjoy a drink that resembled hot, murky water.

"Morning," Yvonne called from the lounge as she passed into the dining room.

"Morning," she replied, a little croaky where her voice had not yet woken up.

She made herself some toast and joined her mum and sister in the lounge. When she entered she felt as though

196

they had finished whatever conversation they were having because of her being there. She ignored the atmosphere and looked over at Jake who was amusing himself with the title sequence of *Rugrats* on the television. She may have been too old for cartoons but she shared Jake's eclectic taste in them.

The back door was open but Jake was obviously put off by what had happened the night before and had chosen to stay indoors. She didn't blame him. No one really knew what had happened when he was up there as not only did they not want to make too much of a drama out of it, but they also found it hard to understand what he was trying to say when he was upset.

"Do you want to go play up the garden, Jake?" Steph asked as she stood and walked over to the back door, slipping on a pair of flip flops that were left there.

He did not say anything but stood up and walked over to his aunt. He probably did not want to go up there, but he would have more than likely stepped through a burning building if Steph had suggested it.

They stepped out into the south-facing garden which felt like a sun-trap. It was eleven o'clock and you could have cooked an egg on the patio it was so warm. Steph rolled a large, blue plastic paddling pool round from the sideway of the house. It was not that big but had a small plastic slide moulded into the side. Jake's face lit up.

"Stay here and I'll go find your swimming trunks," Steph said as she left Jake sitting cross-legged in the empty pool.

She dashed inside, past Jane and Yvonne and out into the garage to the ironing basket where she knew a pair of cute red swim trunks were that she had bought Jake whilst she had been on shopping trip a couple of weeks earlier. She was not in the garage long before she heard Jake screaming. It was a scream that she recognised, not one which craved attention or even one of pain. It was the same fear-induced cry that she had encountered him make the night before when he had been witness to the ghostly man in the playhouse.

She moved as fast as her legs would carry her, nearly taking the door to the garage off its hinges as she pushed through it. He mother and sister were already on their feet and making their way out into the garden. As she jumped the small step at the back door, her eyes searched the garden to find where Jake was standing thinking that he must be back at the Wendy house or just anywhere that was not where she had left him, but he was. He was still sat in the empty paddling pool, alone. When she had left him he was sitting cross-legged and at ease with his surroundings. Now, his knees were bent up to his chin with his face resting on them. He had his elbows pointing outwards and his hands pressed firmly against his ears.

Steph looked at Yvonne as Jane rushed over to Jake and tried to pick him up.

"Jake, whatever's the matter?" Jane asked, her voice staying calm for the sake of her son who appeared to have lost it entirely.

As she touched his shoulders, the small boy flipped out, punching and kicking, his eyes still tightly shut. "No! No! Tell them to stop! Tell them to stop!" He repeated again and again.

Yvonne ran to his side and both women spent close to five minutes trying to calm Jake from his terrified behaviour which was completely out of character. Eventually he opened his eyes, and allowed himself to calm down seeing both his mum and nan stood in front of him. He held out his arms and Jane embraced him. He laid his head down on her shoulder as he quietly sobbed. Steph just stood, frozen, now staring beyond her nephew who was being marched inside the house.

Steph's attention had settled towards the back of the garden, next to the small shed that sat up high in the right-hand corner. It was an outer building that was used to store garden necessities like the lawnmower and garden chairs. In front of it, about forty feet away from where she was standing was a small flower bed which her mother had filled with a multitude of colours bursting from white hydrangeas, lavender sweet peas and a beautiful, well-watered pink hydrangea bush. It was a gardeners maze of plants, but there stood within it, right in the heart of the maze, a small girl, no older than maybe six or seven years old. She was wearing the same old fashioned attire that she had been wearing when Steph had seen her last in the back bedroom of the house. The difference now was that Steph knew that who she was seeing was in fact a ghost. Before she thought perhaps the vision had been part of a dream, but now she knew that the little girl must be a ghostly image, the same as the man who she had been seeing. The figure was as clear an image as a real person, formed entirely—not a translucent form that films and fiction inform us that spirits look like. The child in front of Steph looked as real as her own reflection did in the mirror.

Steph was frozen to the spot, she could not move. Her legs felt stiff as her whole body was emerged into a state of awe, transfixed on the image in front of her. She could still hear Jake sobbing quietly in the background, Jane trying to probe out of him what the matter was, but all she could concentrate on was the little girl who had not taken her eyes from the paddling pool, a grin appearing on the girl's face.

"Steph! Steph?" She heard Jane coming up behind her. She had more than likely been calling her for longer than she had heard but it took a while for her to be pulled from her hypnotised state. "Steph? We think Jake may speak to you about what just happened, if anything actually did. You know what he's like, probably doing it so that you'd hurry up and play with him."

Steph knew Jake would not do anything like that, but she also knew that Jane was trying to play the situation down so that she could still go out. She lost Jane's attention for just a second and looked back over at the bed of flowers at the back of the garden where the young girl was standing, but as Steph had already guessed, she was gone.

She had not felt danger or threatened by the apparition. In fact she had felt oddly calmed by her presence, and the whole event was tranquil. She turned and walked into the lounge, where Jake was sitting with Yvonne, as he was kissing Jane goodbye. Jane assured that she would not be long and headed on her way. When she was gone, Steph took Jake back into the lounge, put *Rugrats* back on the television and waited whilst Yvonne made them both some toast—whilst also giving Steph some time to see if she could get any more out of Jake who had gone quiet about the situation.

"Are you going to tell me what happened?" Steph asked, acting as though she was making small talk with the child, whilst she took out some of his toys from his wooden toy box. "Was it that man again? The one like the picture on my book?"

Jake never took his eyes from the television as he shook his head.

"Did you see a little girl?" She asked, still moving about the lounge, setting up a game for them to play, making the conversation she was sparking up appear to be blasé. However, the mention of the little girl caught Jake's attention as he turned to look at his aunt. "I saw her too," Steph said, "I think she's a nice little girl isn't she?"

For a child, Jake was thoughtful and although his speech was impaired, he always considered the things that people said to him, which for a two year old, was impressive.

"I like the wittle girl with the wunny blue hat," Jake said, mixing some of his letters with w's. "But there was two girls and a boy and the little boy was being horrible to the wittle girl with the hat."

Three children? Steph thought to herself, she had only ever seen one. She did not want to probe further. Jake was more than likely going to have nightmares for weeks because of the last couple of days so she let the situation turn back to playing games and the possible talk of a water fight as Yvonne walked in the room with toast, cereals and glasses of orange juice. She looked at Steph wanting to know whether she knew any more about what had happened in the garden, so Steph nodded to suggest that she did but now was not the time to discuss it.

They spent the next few hours playing and keeping Jake occupied, not leaving him alone for a moment.

*****

Steph had asked for her mum not to tell anyone about her paranormal experiences. After Lucy's reaction she was worried that others may behave in a similar way, or worse still, they may not believe her. So when Jane stopped by to pick up Jake on her way home from shopping, Yvonne told Jane that they had not found out anything else from him and that it was probably best to talk about things that would take his mind off of the incident. Whether Jane took heed from this or not was a different matter but she agreed whilst downing yet another cup of strong, black coffee and then made her way home.

Eric had told Yvonne that he would be home late. His football team had a presentation night that no doubt would consist of drunken behaviour and a stripper that had seen better days. So Yvonne suggested to Steph that they hire a movie from the local video shop in Sawbridgeworth town and eat lots of junk food. Steph loved spending time with her Mum and agreed so long as the film was of her choice. Surprisingly Steph chose a non-horror genre, *Braveheart*, as it was one that she knew her mum wanted to watch. Whilst serving up numerous amounts of pizza and salad,

Yvonne casually jumped to what had happened earlier in the day.

"You said you'd tell me later, at least that's what you implied. So what happened?" Yvonne asked, handing two full plates to Steph to take into the lounge as she followed her with several bags of monster munch crisps, "What did Jake tell you?"

Steph had no intention of holding back from her mum, she had a right to know what was happening inside her home. She told her about the young girl that she had seen, standing at the back of the garden, watching them and that she had recognised her from a night that she had been awoken in the house a few years previous. She explained what the girl had looked like and what she had been wearing.

"So the clothes looked old?" Yvonne asked, interested.

"They didn't look old like she needed to wash them but like they were from the early twentieth century, I'd say going by history class at school. Mr Briggins would have a field day," Yvonne looked perplexed, "my history teacher," Steph explained.

"Weren't you scared? If what you think you saw was a ghost, didn't it frighten you?"

"It did the first time because I could not talk about it, I was afraid as well because I didn't know what or who she was but knowing that she might be a ghost made me feel more sad than I felt afraid," Steph explained, walking out of the dining room and through to the lounge.

"And you're sure that she was a ghost? Not an actual child or just your..."

Yvonne hesitated, as Steph finished her sentence, "Imagination?" Steph laughed, "Jake saw her too and you didn't see her so yes, I am certain that what I saw today was a ghost. Jake also told me that he saw other children in the garden, one of them wasn't as nice as the girl who I've encountered. He said that he was frightened by him."

202

Yvonne's face lost all expression, the corners of her lips dropped and the pupils in her eyes dilated, "What do you mean he saw other children in the garden?"

"When I asked him if it was the little girl who had frightened him, he told me that he saw a little girl but also two other children. Mum, I think this place is proper haunted. Who lived here before us?"

For a moment Yvonne considered telling her daughter about the old lady she had met fourteen years ago in Sawbridgeworth library and about the tale she was told that there was once a fire in Sawbridgeworth, near Greenmay Close that had killed several children and animals but she believed that her daughter had experienced enough and would hold on to the information until the time was right.

"Does Dad know anything?" Steph asked, her voice high-pitched and full of enthusiasm, excited to be opening up after so long.

"No, he doesn't and I would prefer for it to stay that way, for now. Look, Nanny Ellen is coming to stay in a couple of weeks and once she's settled in, I would like for you to tell her about your experiences, ask her any questions you might have and see what she thinks about your psychic ability."

"Psychic?" Steph retorted, her voice humouring her mother, "I'm not psychic!" She said, laughing. *Why did everyone think that?*

"You are more than most. How many of your friends see dead children in their gardens?" Yvonne said, her face half amused, half terrified by the statement. "Speak to Nanny, let's see what she thinks. And for God sake, if I've learned anything during my life, it's not to mess with things we don't understand so please, promise me, you won't antagonise any of the spirits that you see. Don't speak to them, look at them or try to contact them when you can't see them. Leave them be." Yvonne asked, begged of her daughter knowing all too well what could happen if you dabbled with the dead.

It was a statement, and not one that needed an answer but Steph gave one anyway, "I promise."

Chapter twenty-three. Visitor.

It was a few weeks before Ellen visited and during which time activity at Greenmay Close seemed to go quiet. They never kept a log or diary of the paranormal events but they were all aware of it, even Eric who tried to ignore it. Steph was always the most affected, whether that was because of her age (research suggests that females reaching puberty are the most susceptible to paranormal activity) or because she opened herself up to it, no-one was sure. Things still went missing—a hairbrush, money—but they would always turn up later, sometimes in the same place that they thought they had left them days before, or sometimes somewhere entirely obscure like in the refrigerator or hiding at the back of a wardrobe or cupboard.

Jake however had complained about something a little more serious. It was Jane who approached Yvonne about the subject.

"Jake had one of his night terrors last night," she told her mum on the phone one Saturday morning, "but it was different to the others. It seemed like it affected him this time."

"What happened?" Yvonne asked, as she made herself comfortable on the small two-seater sofa they had in the dining room.

Jake had been suffering from night terrors for a few months. They usually involved dreams that had him running away from someone, being chased or some other cat-and-mouse type escapade. The doctors had said that it was fairly common in young children and that it was nothing to worry about.

"He came into Gareth and I at about two o'clock in the morning, sobbing. His forehead was sweating buckets, like he was running a fever. I thought he was coming down with something, like stomach flu, but besides the fever, he had no other symptoms. I tried to calm him down. Gareth went to his bedroom to find Gummy—his bear—" Yvonne knew the toy Jane was referring to, "but when he came back into the bedroom, his face was white and he looked ill himself."

"Why?" Yvonne asked, her mind frantically trying to explore every possibility.

"Well, at the time he didn't say but when Jake had calmed down enough to talk, he was going on and on about a woman in his bed that had tried to kill him."

"What!" Yvonne stood back to her feet, "What the hell did he mean?"

"Mum, calm down. Gareth confirmed that there was no one in his bedroom. Jake insisted that the woman had put her hands around his throat and he couldn't breathe. But the weirdest thing Mum, is that when I checked his neck, there were red marks around it like someone really had tried to strangle him." Jane began to cry.

"Give me five minutes, and I'll come over."

*****

Within thirty minutes, Yvonne was stood at Jane's front door. The young family had moved out into the country, closer to Saffron Walden and had found a house out in the sticks with only one other neighbour in a two mile radius. The house was maybe one hundred years old, with several tiny rooms downstairs that they did not use. Too many nooks-and-crannies for most people's likings, but Jane had loved the land and scarcity of the place. But in a time of need, it was never any good to anyone being miles from civilisation.

"Where is he?" She asked, looking past Jane who was hovering in the doorway.

"He's asleep, thank goodness. Gareth and I are really freaked out. He's just popped out to do the shopping. I said that I would stay with Jake to let him sleep."

"I'm not surprised when Jake's been having such awful nightmares. No wonder his imagination is so irrational sometimes," Yvonne said, making her way in to the lounge, "Tell me again what Jake says happened."

Jane went on to explain how they had been woken by their son, that he had been uncontrollably crying as he described an elderly woman who had supposedly tried to strangle him. He had described her as wearing all black and a net in front of her face. He said that she had skin that was cracked and bubbled in places.

"Obviously we put it down to just another night terror but when Gareth went into Jake's bedroom to check that everything was OK, he said that the place looked as though it had been ransacked. Honestly Mum, everything was everywhere. His bed sheets were on the floor, drawers and wardrobe had been emptied out. There's just no way he could have done it himself. Someone else must have been in there." Jane's eyes started to well up. "I've never seen Gareth look so worried which only made me feel worse." Jane had never been good at hiding her emotions and that day had been no different.

"It's OK," Yvonne said, trying to comfort her daughter, "I'm sure it was just a nightmare. He could have been sleep walking and caused the mess. There are lots of explanations that could have caused his distress. No one else was in the house, so there isn't any other explanation."

"But what about what happened at yours last weekend? When he was saying that he could hear and see people in your garden; I'm getting really worried. What if he can see people like Granddad could?"

Yvonne had her arms around her daughter's shoulders. She did not have anything else to say to her, no more words of comfort to give. She too, was worried, scared for Jake's sake. She knew too that what Jake had been seeing were spirits, especially with the descriptions that Steph had also given. It was too much of a coincidence to be anything else, but now that he was getting attacked physically, it was becoming a cause for concern.

"You need to play the situation down, you don't want to upset him any more than what he is already. Try to make light of it," Yvonne suggested. "But over the next few days, watch him, monitor his behaviour and if anything else happens or he gets any more anxious about what has already happened, besides seeing a doctor, perhaps you need to get help from the church."

The Camp's had never been practicing Christians but they were all Christians with faith resting in God. "It's my only other suggestion."

They could hear Jake upstairs, calling for Jane. They spent the rest of the morning playing and taking Jacob's mind off of the events that took place the night before. Yvonne hoped that he was still young enough to not dwell on it for too long, but for them, they would not find such events as easy to forget.

*****

It was the week after Steph turned thirteen that Ellen came to stay. A week had passed since Jake had been visited by the woman in his bed, and both Steph and Yvonne were keen to speak to Ellen. Steph was particularly eager since finding out that the granddad she never knew was a Medium—or something similar. Yvonne had told Eric what had happened to Jake and although he believed her, he always tried rationalising a situation before running off with the notion that there was a haunting or ghosts to blame. Growing up in 106 Poultney Road, he knew all too well that once you start letting paranormal entities affect your thoughts, they end up taking over your life so he preferred to offer logic where possible and settled with Jake's experience being a night terror. It might well have

208

been, but what happens when the nightmares start happening when you are awake?

Yvonne suggested to Steph that they let her nan settle in before bombarding her with stories of ghosts and hauntings, and so spent the first night of Ellen's stay watching game shows and episodes of *Coronation Street*. They all went to bed fairly early and Steph woke up just before eight o'clock the next morning. Yvonne and Ellen were already downstairs in the lounge with the Sunday newspapers sprawled across the floor.

Steph wandered into the two women, Ellen a little more engrossed in the story she was reading than Yvonne who jumped at the sight of Steph, "Christ, you made me jump!" Yvonne said, startled.

Ellen looked up, a smile sweeping across her face, "Good morning my beautiful girl, did you sleep OK?"

Finding it an odd question for her nan to be asking her now that she was thirteen and had not had a problem sleeping since being a toddler, she answered "Fine, thanks, Nan. You?"

Ellen looked over at Yvonne, who was standing from the sofa, "I'm going to leave you two to talk," she said, smiling at her daughter and closing the door on her way out.

Steph knew immediately that something had happened and that perhaps her mother had already given Ellen the heads up on the weird occurrences that her and her nephew had experienced over the past few years.

She wanted to tell her nan everything, "So has Mum told you?"

Ellen smiled, "In fact, it was me who brought up the subject this morning."

Steph said nothing.

"Ghosts. Spirits. About this house and about you. Last night I went to bed without so much of considering that this house was haunted. Normally I'm pretty good at determining whether or not there is activity in a house. It's what comes when you've lived amongst the dead for so many years, but I've stayed here so many times without anything occurring that I never thought that there would be anything untoward here. That was until last night."

Steph was still quiet. The conversation had taken an unexpected turn and she was intrigued.

"I woke up at around three o'clock to go for a piddle. I do every night so nothing took me as unusual but when I got back in to bed I just couldn't sleep. I never have problems sleeping here, not like I do at home. Living by yourself can be creepy sometimes. But here, surrounded by family, I usually sleep like a baby. Not last night. I tossed and turned for what seemed like hours and then I felt her. Not physically, I could feel a presence in the room with me. It's like someone is watching, like there's no escape from their grip," she never took her eyes from her granddaughter. "But you know that already don't you? What it's like to feel haunted? The temperature was colder than usual so I had the duvet pulled up high, but not high enough. I didn't have long to think about what was happening before I felt her icy hand on my bare shoulder. Like you, I didn't scream, I didn't even feel all that frightened, as although the touch was clearly not human. It was somewhat similar to touching a piece of meat that had been in the refrigerator - cold and a bit slimy you know? Well, I didn't feel threatened." Without realising, Steph had shifted towards the edge of her seat, holding her breath and so intent on hearing her Nan's story that she had even forgotten to breathe.

"I turned over to see what or who it was standing there but instead of being stood beside my bed where I had expected her to be, she had moved simultaneously as I did, over to the door. Ghosts can do that, they don't need to follow you or stay static, they can move as fast as light. I don't know why but I have always presumed it's because they have no substance, no body or time. They defy

210

everything that the living try to rationalise. They are everything that logic is not. If we listened to science and theories from scientists, sceptics or atheists, then the likes of you and I, and particularly Granddad Dick, would end up in a loony bin." Ellen smiled, "I saw her too. The little girl wearing the blue and white pinafore dress and mop hat? She visited me last night. I told Yvonne this morning and she said that you and Jake are the only ones who have seen her, but she also told me something else. Something that I think you need to hear."

Yvonne came walking back into the lounge, fresh cup of coffee in hand and a hot, milky cup of tea for Ellen. She sat down with her daughter and told her about the woman she had met in the library, about the fire years ago that had killed several children and animals on farm land which was replaced by the houses on Greenmay Close. She told her about the gravestone of the young girl that was found in the building structure of the house and that the previous owners had taken it with them when they moved.

"I don't think the little girl can pass over. I think her soul is lost because she has no way of knowing that she is dead. No place to rest. But Steph, you must understand that it's not your place to try to save her or understand her turmoil. It can be very dangerous to get involved in the paranormal and in the explanations of it." Ellen's tone changed, her face becoming harder, "Your Mum mentioned that you have seen another ghost? A man?"

Steph swallowed hard and nodded.

"Tell me about him," Ellen asked.

Steph continued to tell her nan about the time that Jake had been attacked in the garden and when she had looked, they both had seen a tall figure in the playhouse, dressed in black. Ellen asked to describe what he looked like, and Steph told her, "Tall, wearing a black coat and a tall black hat."

211

"And you could see this though the small window in that little house?" Ellen asked, pointing out towards the garden.

Steph sat for a moment, "No Nan, I saw him at your house too."

"At Poultney Road?" Yvonne asked, putting down the cup of luke-warm coffee.

"No, in your new house. The day you moved in. I saw a dog that could have been Prince, and then when I looked up at your house from the garden, I saw the same man looking down at me from your spare room window. I'm so sorry I didn't say anything at the time, I didn't want people to think I was making it up."

Ellen took a deep breath. "My dear girl, you must be careful of this entity. Unlike the small girl who haunts this house, the man in black doesn't haunt a house, he's not trapped because his spirit can't rest. He's caught in limbo because he wants to be here. For so many years, Richard believed that he haunted him and would follow him into the afterlife when he died. For so many years he tried to protect me from him but he never wanted Richard. I think he wants me. He connected to Richard as a boy because he could, because your grandfather had a degree of psychic ability, he could connect with the dead—I couldn't. I now know that he used Richard's ability to find me."

"How do you know that, Ellen?" Yvonne asked. "How do you know that he didn't leave the family when Richard died? That what Steph is seeing isn't something else?"

"I know," Ellen said, "because I see him too."

Chapter twenty-four. Enough is enough.

The night of Richard's death was the first of many that Ellen would be visited by the man in black. For the first few months she put much of the paranormal phenomena down to grief, but once life had otherwise returned to normal, and the apparitions and paranormal occurrences remained, she could no longer blame them on the loss of her husband. Over the years she had grown accustomed to the sound of people talking and the echoes of children crying in the hallway. Most of the time these experiences came and went on a weekly, sometimes daily basis and she knew that these spirits haunted the house on Poultney Road, they did not haunt her. Knowing this comforted her, knowing that eventually, when she had the courage, she would be able to move away from them and live a life free from tormented souls. However, the man in black was one entity that she never understood. He had manifested in locations outside the house.

She had spent many years asking herself who he was and what he wanted. Whether he had contributed to the death of Richard's childhood friend, Harry or whether his first sighting was just bad timing. About six months after Richard's death, Ellen had become obsessed with the paranormal and with the life that Richard had tried to protect her from. She made a diary going right back to when Richard told her about the first paranormal sighting that he remembered baring witness to the day that Harry died. From then she remembered that Harry came to him, that he had visited him in the night and talked to him, asking for help or some kind of resolution. She remembered the first time that she had bared witness to paranormal activity and that had been inside 106 Poultney Road when Richard showed her a photograph that he had taken at a wedding in the church graveyard which clearly showed the little red-headed boy. Harry's ghost had been the only other one besides the man in black which seemed to linger, who could not rest in peace. Her son, Eric had seen him several times as a boy and she knew that the crying she often heard in the early hours belonged to him.

She wanted to try to finish what her husband had started. She wanted to put the lost souls trapped inside that house out of their misery and help them pass over.

*****

It was shortly before Yvonne went into labour with Steph at the end of autumn 1983 that Ellen had attended a local psychic fare. There were people she could have asked to get involved in the séance she was planning on having. Friends whom Richard often turned to for his meetings of Ouija boards and séances, but she decided that she wanted to bring fresh minds into her meeting, a group who had no presumptions of the house or its inhabitants. Ellen was a very friendly cockney woman who was loved by pretty much everyone she knew so making friends was not hard for her. She got chatting to an older couple who sat next to her during the show, which was rather staged and uncomfortable for Ellen to watch. She had nothing against psychics but it took more than their private show of contact to prove to her that they had made a connection. Mostly due to the amount of shared experiences that she had witnessed with her husband.

The couple were Betty and John Dorling. They were quiet in their mannerisms and had kept themselves to themselves until Ellen introduced herself and they got talking. They lived in a small village north of Essex called Colchester. They both had loved ones they had lost over the years and had gained interest in psychic meetings and gatherings after losing their son in a motor bike accident eight years earlier. Ellen told them that she was new to the paranormal game and was keen to hold a séance at her home. The couple were eager to get involved and asked if they could invite their friends, Margaret and Billy Turner. Ellen obviously agreed, it increased her participant level and a date was set.

The front bedroom upstairs in 106 Poultney Road had bared witness to its fair share of paranormal activity over the years and she was optimistic that the evening would reacquaint them. She had every intention of doing good and to hopefully let a few lost souls rest but with absolutely no experience of hosting such meetings, all she could go by was what she remembered from the minimal meetings she attended of Richard's.

Her guests arrived together just after seven o'clock on the evening of September twenty-eight, 1983. Margaret and Billy were the most eager of the two couples, and introduced themselves upon arrival at Poultney Road.

"You must be Ellen?" Billy asked as Ellen pulled open the large wooden front door of her home, "Thank you so much for inviting us this evening. Margaret and I have attended so many meetings over the years," he talked whilst walking into the hallway downstairs. Betty, John and his wife followed in closely behind, not getting a word in edgeways. "We have sat back for the past few years and have attended less active meetings and opted for the psychic nights instead. We really are excited about tonight aren't we Marg?"

Whether or not the question was rhetorical, Margaret replied, her eyes bright and voice slightly louder than she probably intended, "Very excited indeed. Will you be hosting?"

"Yes, I will be hosting this evening and I'm not sure whether or not Betty or John have mentioned it, but this will be the first meeting I have hosted," the guests looked at one another, bewildered.

"Then, why now?" Billy asked, saying what everyone else was thinking.

"I lost my husband, Richard nine months ago and I long to contact him. I also strongly believe that this house has an uninvited lodger. A little boy called Harry. I have seen what could be his spirit many times over the years, heard him cry, he moves things. You know, the usual paranormal activity," Ellen spoke fast, almost dismissing the interest her guests would obviously have in her story, she wanted to give them as little background information as possible but enough for them to understand the things she may say during the séance. "I think I need to help the child's soul rest. It's as though he is trapped here. Perhaps taken suddenly?"

None of the guests said anything in reply. Billy was looking about the hallway, obviously trying to get a feel for the place, either that or just being plain nosey. The other three all looked at Ellen, waiting for their next instruction.

"We will hold the séance upstairs, in the front bedroom as this is where I have experienced the most activity from Harry," Ellen began to lead her guests upstairs, she already sensed a presence as she pulled her knitted cardigan tighter around her bust, and tried to ignore the dense atmosphere that lingered in the upper part of the house. It didn't bother Ellen anymore; she had grown accustomed to the oddities of the house, the same way a couple grows used to the strange habits they discover of their partner after marriage. Some things have to be ignored or it can tear you apart at the seams.

"I hope you don't mind me asking but, how do you know that this child's ghost belongs to a boy named Harry?" Betty asked, rubbing her hands up and down the length of her upper arms.

Ellen thought briefly, not quite knowing how to answer without giving too much away, "Because I've dreamt of him. I think he comes to me when I sleep."

216

Her guests took what Ellen told them as gospel and followed her along the long, narrow landing to the bedroom at the front of the house. They passed Flo's room, the door was shut and no doubt she had taken herself to bed early. She had told Ellen earlier at dinner that she was tired and would retire to bed before her guests arrived.

The front room was empty and sparse. The large inglenook fireplace was lost amongst the tall ceiling and lack of furniture. In an old house, the fireplace was the only piece of character it had in the room. Ellen felt the drop in temperature as they entered so she knew that her guests must have felt it too.

"I'm sure you know the procedure better than I do but I will ask that we all hold hands and not break the connection until I say it's OK to do so. Should you wish to leave before we have finished then I would ask that you tell me so that we can end with a prayer."

The lighting was dull inside the room with only a couple of wall lamps to brighten the space. There had been a tall floor lamp but it had smashed a couple of months before Richard had passed away during his last meeting with the dead and Ellen had never gotten around to replacing it.

Everyone held hands and stood in silence for a moment.

"If anyone is there, please give us a sign. If anyone is there, please give us a sign." Ellen began chanting.

Part of her was anxious. Would she contact young Harry and perhaps put his soul to rest or would she connect with Richard? The other part of her conscience worried about the latter of the two scenarios. She knew that he would not be impressed with her tampering with the dead. She remembered the promise which she made to him shortly after his last séance, the last time he had contact with the man in black. She shuddered.

"Please give us a sign, move something, speak, and connect with us. We are not here to harm you. If anyone is there, please give us a sign." She continued with her thoughts somewhere else. She knew that she should be concentrating.

She looked around at her guests, their eyes closed, focused on the purpose, on the possibility of connecting with loved ones and the reassurance that there was, in fact, life after death. But all Ellen could think about was that promise. The promise that at the time of making it, she had every intention of keeping. *Promise me,* Richard had asked. *Promise me that when I die, you won't follow in my footsteps, that nothing and no one could ever make you use a Ouija board or be curious about séances. You must promise me.* The main reason that Ellen had ever submitted to that promise was because she honestly believed that when Richard passed over, when he was no longer with her in a living form that the uninvited occupants of the house would pass over too. A naive synopsis but it is what she told herself, it was what helped her accept what had happened inside her home for so many years. That once the perpetrator left the premises, so too would the intruders. Little had she known that all along, it was her that the man in black wanted. The spirit that had once terrified her husband was simply waiting for the right time to strike. Ellen now knew that that time would never have been when Richard was there to fight her corner.

The bedroom door rattled and Betty lifted her head and opened her eyes. The others soon followed suit as the rattling continued to become more forceful. Ellen continued to speak, "Give us a sign. Give us a sign," all the time thinking that there was the possibility that it could be Flo playing one of her deluded games.

The closed curtains at the window flickered. Ellen faced them and watched as they glided out into the room, swaying and billowing like a window was open and they were dancing with the wind. Even though the night was cool and they had all felt a chill walking through the house earlier, the temperature once again, dropped. But this time goose bumps covering their arms, tightening their senses. As the curtain made a large swoop of the room, Ellen took a quick glimpse behind it to make sure that a window had not been left open. She saw the white frame first, the wooden surround contrasting against the deep wallpaper which was plastered all around it. She saw the edge and then more of the clear, large window which hid itself behind the heavy material. Then, she saw skin, the formation of a small hand. A child's hand. It was clenched into a fist. The curtains swooped further, deeper into the room and almost touching Margaret's hair as she sat with her back to the phenomena, still trying to concentrate on the words that Ellen spoke. Ellen had stopped speaking, her attention had turned to the figure that was showing itself to her. The small hand of a child which rested itself on a dark pair of cotton trousers, his shirt messed and dirty so that you were no longer able to tell it's colour. His hair was still as red as it had looked in the photographs that she had been shown by her late husband. His face had the same, bewildered expression that she had seen in the photograph the first time she had come back to Poultney Road. The photograph that had appeared from nowhere and had been engulfed into a nest of flames. His eyes were dark, not just the brown that you would expect on a little red-headed boy, they were black, the pupils were wide, like marbles, glassy. He watched them, his face effortless, no emotion, no reaction, just a bystander to a much larger game.

"We have a connection," Ellen told the group who were now looking around the room, aware of a presence. "Harry, we are not here to hurt you, we are here to help you."

As she spoke, one of the lights on the wall above her head flickered. "Harry, please don't run away, don't be scared, we want to help you pass over."

Until that point, the curtain had continued to move, Ellen had been reacquainted with the image of the young boy behind it every time that it blew into the room but on her last sentence, the movement stopped. The curtain fell back to its resting place and the room was still. It was silent too, so silent that as soon as the crying began, all five of those involved in the séance, could hear it. It started off quietly, coming from the curtains at the front of the room. Ellen had caught sight of Margaret who had perspiration building up on her forehead. The room was still freezing cold but obviously her nerves were getting the better of her. Ellen knew she must stay strong, resolve the situation if she was ever to rid herself of her haunting.

"Harry is that you?" The gentle crying soon turned to a slightly louder sob. Like a child hurt or injured. "Show yourself to me again, Harry, let the others here see who it is that they are speaking too."

The sobbing got louder and the handle on the door began to shake again, twisting as though someone on the other side of it was eager to get in. Ellen tried to hide the fear from her voice but it was difficult when she already knew that Harry's ghost was already in the room with them which meant that he either wanted to get out or someone else was trying to get in.

"Who's there, playing with the door handle?" Billy called into the room, "Come in! Come in and show yourself!" He cried out.

Ellen gasped as the light above her head, the bulb of which had been flickering for most part of the séance, smashed, some of the glass only just missing her face. The light at the far end of the wall did little to brighten the room and left the door in a shadow of the guests. It too started to flicker. Whilst their attention was focused upon the broken light, they had forgotten all about the door handle, which now had fallen silent. Silent because it had been turned fully, releasing the catch. It creaked quietly, pushing itself open.

Betty gasped, "Something doesn't feel right," she announced but no one paid her any attention.

The one thing you can rely on with those of us who are interested in the paranormal, is that it does not take a lot to convince us that supernatural phenomenon is occurring, but once the entity has our attention, we are in it for the long haul. When they have waited years to experience such things, it would take a lot for them to run from the situation without seeing it through. Ellen knew she had made the right choice as she looked at the four guest's faces, full of fear and anticipation, eager to see more.

They all looked at the door which had opened about eighteen inches, enough for someone to be able to fit through. They heard the floor boards creak around the circle that they were still occupying. One step, two step. It passed John who was squeezing Ellen's hand tightly. The third step was slow, the board creaked and then kept its unbalanced position beneath whatever it was holding it down. Whatever or whoever it was in the room with them, was stood directly behind Ellen.

She had not realised that she had been holding her breath and when she released it, her breath turned in a foggy mist, like a cloud of smoke after inhaling a long chug of tobacco, but there was no cigarette, no pipe, just the icy air that encased them all.

Possibly more nervous than any of the others, Ellen's body tightened. She knew who it was that had made its way in with them. She was used to the change of atmosphere, when it became dark and heavy. She was used to the damp air and plummeting temperatures. She knew that when the goose pimples covered her body that he was there. The man in black.

Her hair was short which bared her neck and she felt a short, sharp gush of icy air blow upon her skin. She flinched at the sensation and at the vile stench that had filled the room. John gripped her hand tighter. She could not breathe, she could not move because she knew that he would follow her wherever she went. The dim light

221

alongside from their circle stopped flickering, she felt herself breathe out although she was no longer aware of her actions. She dropped her hand from John's grip.

"Ellen!" John whispered into the dark.

"Please," Ellen whispered, "wait here for one minute. If I don't come back then leave, but give me a minute."

The group stood in silence as they listened to her footsteps running out of the room and along the landing. They heard her try to flick a light switch somewhere deeper in the house. "Damn," they heard her small voice curse. Within no more than thirty seconds they saw a flashlight fill the landing with Ellen's hand gripped tightly around it. In her other hand she had another torch, a larger one which she handed to Billy. All of the guests still held on to one another's hands.

"You can let go, the circle is useless in this house," the four friends stood looking at Ellen, "the ghosts were already here, I don't think a circle is going to help the evil that already resides here. Now," she said, pulling out a board from underneath her arm, "who's tried a Ouija board?" Ellen asked, feeling hopeful. One by one, all of her guests nodded. "OK, we need to speak to whoever or whatever it is that haunts this house. Are you all OK with this?"

Billy spoke, "I am, but I just wish you had prepared us more. I thought we were coming here to connect with loved ones we've lost over the years. Starting something new not dabbling with an existing haunting."

"I'm sorry," Ellen said, "I was scared that none of you would want to help me if you knew. Please, I ask you to stay for just a while, just to see if we can help whatever it is trapped inside this house."

Again, they all nodded.

Ellen forced a smile, "Thank you. Can we start by sitting on the floor?"

They all followed instruction. One-by-one they sat themselves down in a circle, both Ellen and Billy holding on tightly to their torches, the beam of light shaking as their hands trembled. Once on her knees, Ellen placed the wooden board in the centre of them all and took the planchette out of her cardigan pocket, placing it on the board.

"Please all put the tip of your right index finger on the edge of the planchette," All five people did as they were told. The room was still dark besides the torch light, which lit up the board in front of them and not much else. "We know that you are there," Ellen spoke gently, her voice shaky, "we ask that you come in peace. We mean you no harm and would like to help you."

Billy's torch light started to flicker. He shook it, smacking the head of it against his knee to reacquaint the room with its comforting glow.

"Who are you?" Ellen asked, her voice stronger than before, "we know you're there. I have known for years that you have resided in this property. We are here to help you."

Ellen's voice was interrupted by the sudden dash of the wooden planchette beneath her finger. The group all jumped in unison as though they had experienced a simultaneous shock through their bodies. It slid over to read **NO**.

Ellen asked, "OK. So you don't want our help?"

The planchette flew around the board in a circle back to the same place, **NO**.

"You don't want to be able to rest in peace?" Ellen asked again, her voice stern.

NO.

"Why do you want to stay here?" She said into the darkness, the eyes of her guests not moving from the board.

Billy's flash light went out.

"Why do you want to stay here?"

223

The planchette started spinning, around and around the board, its speed building up as though it was getting ready to launch.

E.L.L.E.N

It was the first time that the guests all looked away from the board and at their host. The colour had drained from her face like someone suffering with anaemia, the black circles beneath her blue eyes exaggerated by the insipidness of her skin. No one spoke as they all felt the planchette begin to shake beneath their finger tips.

Perspiration trickled down the side of John's temple, tickling his senses as he reached with his right hand to scratch away the sensation, letting go of his connection with the planchette. Before anyone had the chance to respond, to react to his mistake, they all heard a smacking sound, and watched as John's head shifted from right to left as though someone had hit him across the face, hard. He screamed out, shocked by the sensation.

"Put your finger back on the planchette, John," Betty called out as the door of the room slammed shut behind them.

Ellen turned quickly to see who was there and in the shadow of the room, she saw him. She quickly turned back to the board.

"Are there spirits trapped in this house because of you? Are you preventing poor Harry's ghost from passing?"

Ellen had always questioned why Harry would want to come back to haunt his former best friend but she thought that maybe he had come back to protect him and was now trapped with the living because of a much stronger, darker entity.

The planchette was circling the board, **YES**.

The planchette continued to circle, and as though from speakers around the room, there was a roar of laughter, a deep, crackling resonance that would haunt the five participants until their dying days.

224

W.A.I.T.I.N.G F.O.R. E.L.L.E.N

Before they had time to say aloud what the board had spelt, the planchette rose from beneath their touch and flew across the room, mid-air, hitting the wall next to the fireplace. The second and final torch went out, leaving the room in darkness and in silence.

Margaret screamed and was the first of the four to leave the room, running as fast as her legs would take her. The other three guests all rose to their feet and within seconds had made it downstairs and outside where the streetlamps were brighter than the darkness that lingered inside the house. Ellen however, remembered that Flo was still asleep in her room at the end of the hall. Running to the top of the stairs, she paused, letting the four visitors overtake her. She tried the door knob of her mother-in-laws room, it turned effortlessly.

The room overlooked the station at the back of the house which Ellen knew would be well lit so she marched across the darkened room and pulled open the curtains. She was then able to see clearly but she had not expected to see what awaited her. Lying in the bed soundly was Flo. The duvet was pulled up high around her face as she lay, breathing steadily, a mist of cold fog leaving her mouth every few seconds. Standing at the foot of her bed was a shadowy figure that she recognised.

He looked much younger than when she had seen him last and it was as though the cancer had yet to devour his body. His hair was thick and his skin smooth. His eyes somewhat darker than Ellen remembered as they gazed into hers. Richard smiled at his wife and looked down at a small child who was standing by his side. A red headed boy who she also recognised. Harry. They had found each other. Against all odds and against the will of darkness, they had been reunited.

Ellen felt the tears build in her eyes and gush down her cheek like water cascading down a waterfall. Her legs beneath her weight turned to jelly and she collapsed onto the floor and watched as the image of her late husband took one last look at his mother's resting body and disappeared into nothingness.

Ellen did not move as she heard the footsteps of people running up the stairs of her house. She did not move when the light in the landing came on and a policeman entered the room. She did not move when they checked on Flo who was shaken from her sleep and only allowed herself to be moved because she did not have the strength to fight it.

Betty, John, Margaret and Billy had got the police. None of them had wanted to re-enter the house but had been fearful for Ellen who was still inside. All of them had witnessed the events that took place that night and although all of them had witnessed paranormal activity before, none of them had expected what they had seen and heard the night they visited Poultney Road. They made their promises to Ellen that they would keep in touch but none of them ever did.

The police did their job and checked that there had been no foul play, no signs of forced entry and that no-one was hurt and then too, left the scene. They had offered to take Ellen to family or a friend for the night but she did not want to be anywhere but Poultney Road. She knew that Richard's spirit had been there, if only for a moment or two and that was enough to subside the fear that she felt about the man in black who she knew also waited for her inside the house.

*****

Ellen often wondered why the man in black would want to haunt the living for her sake. Why he chose not to rest because of her. What baffled her more than anything else was that he had haunted Richard long before he had met her. So how would he have known that the two of them

226

would ever meet? It was unfortunately something that she never lived long enough to understand.

From that night on she never heard Harry's woeful cries again, she never experienced the frustrating poltergeist behaviour that he had continued for many years during his haunting. She knew it was because somehow, the séance she had held that night with the four strangers whom she would never meet again, somehow connected to her husband's wandering spirit. Harry was able to find Richard amongst the darkness whilst the evil that possessed the house was distracted, and he was finally able to pass over.

She was also never again visited by her late husband. Besides that one night, no one ever saw Richard's ghost. For so many years he had promised to prove life continued after death, *when I die,* he would jokingly say, *I will haunt you all.* But he never did, unless, you may believe, he chose to come back through his granddaughter, Stephanie, who was born less than a month after Ellen's first and last attempt at hosting a séance.

Epilogue

My Nan passed away when I was twenty-one, nine years ago. Cancer plagued her body plummeting her weight by half of her healthy size. She refused to go to hospital or even to have tests, but from a post mortem after her death they found that she had cancer of the stomach, breast and in her head. My Nanny Ellen was one of the bravest women I have ever met and I pray that now, she too, has returned to her former, healthier ways before she got sick, similarly to how she had described seeing Richard nine months after he passed.

Since Ellen's death, none of my family have seen her spirit, my Granddad Richard, Harry or the man in black. The latter one troubles me somewhat. When I was told about him and how he had haunted my family for decades, I worried that because I had started to see him and so too had Jacob that he had taken to haunting us. I think this is why I chose to dabble with the paranormal. I wanted to find answers to questions that were still left unanswered from my parents and grandparents but it does not always work that way. It's like losing weight, the first place a woman gains weight is on her hips and the last is on her bust, she doesn't get to chose where the weight goes. It's the same with séances and Ouija boards. They allow the living to communicate with the dead, they act as portals to another world and at no point can we chose who at the other end we will connect with. It's a risk and one I would never be prepared to take again.

*****

Learning about my Granddad's past opened up a whole new door to curiosity and interest in a subject matter that already consumed my beliefs. At the age of fourteen I encouraged something among my friends involving a

229

séance in our school field. It was the start of something that took over our lives and my life in particular for the two years that followed. It is a story that I have hidden away in one of those places that gets so deeply buried in your memory that you would need to open up a whole new chapter to find it. My mother took me to several meetings at Stansted Hall to talk about a solution and to see if anything might come through during one of their séances. One evening after one of the lectures, one of the psychics approached me. They told me that they could see a dark aura around me and that something evil followed me. I already knew this, my family and close friends at the time knew it too. We asked them if they could help me, to help free whatever it was that followed me, but they said that I would need to seek professional help from the church. Even though my family had experienced many paranormal occurrences in the past and had more tolerance with such things, my mother was worried that I would live a life like my Granddad Richard and spend it searching for answers and a resolution to every supernatural experience I encountered. She took me to see a priest. We explained what had happened to me and asked if it might be possible for a haunting, on this occasion, not to reside within a house, that in fact, it might be me that was haunted. He advised me that under the circumstances and that a possession had not overtaken my person that I was simply to wear a cross around my neck, keep a bible under my bed and to never, ever talk about the occurrences that took place over those years. Although his advice proved accurate, wearing a cross has been one thing that no matter how big or small, or how expensive it might be, to this day I can't wear one.

My Mum chose a nice gold chain and matching cross from a local jeweller in Sawbridgeworth. I put it on that night but by the next day, it was gone. We searched the house high and low but we never found it. Mum went back to the same shop and purchased yet another. Again I put the cross straight on but by the following evening when I got out of the shower I found that the chain around my neck was missing the pendant that had been attached to it. My mum went back to the jeweller with the chain and told him what had happened which of course, he found hard to believe but suggested soldering the cross to the chain, which he did.

My problem was then not that I was losing the cross but that a red rash appeared on my chest. It was itchy and very sore and within forty-eight hours I got very sick. My mum asked me whether I thought it could be related and I said I wasn't sure but thought I would take it off to see what happened. Low and behold, by the next morning the rash was cleared and the sickness gone.

Recently my husband, Elliott and I moved to a house out in the country and I started to experience certain things that I consider to be paranormal. Things disappearing and reappearing moments later, footsteps on the landing when we are both downstairs and my husband often replies to questions that he thinks I have called out to him when I have not said anything at all, (my husband remains a sceptic). When I told my mum about the occurrences, she panicked and went straight out and bought me a cross. I told Elliott about the last time I had worn one and he laughed at me and told me not to be silly. It was a really pretty piece of jewellery and I put it on straight away at around three o'clock that afternoon. We went home and within a couple of hours I was curled up in bed feeling extremely ill and sick. I vomited twice and then remembered that I had the cross around my neck. I mentioned it to Elliott who was fathomed as much as I was by my sudden illness and suggested I took it off and within an hour or so I was well again.

I would also know if a bible is put under my bed. My Mum tried it a couple of times after the Priest's suggestion but each time, I would spend hours trying tossing and turning and finally know what she had done. One time I remember finding the bible and placing it outside my bedroom door, only to return to bed and drift into a peaceful sleep almost instantly. I've not tried this for years, but one day no doubt, that little bugger known as curiosity will come back around to greet me again.

I have no idea what this means or why it continues to happen to me fifteen years since the last time I dabbled with the paranormal but all I know is that no matter how much I was asked, I would never ever touch a Ouija board again. It's weird though, the poltergeist activity that occurred in my family home continued all the while I lived there and stopped almost the instant I left. Could it be yet another coincidence that I have continued to experience such phenomena in the home I now share with my husband? I guess no one can ever answer me that either.

*****

Before his death, Richard made my parents, my Uncles and Nan promise that they would never follow in his footsteps and play with things they didn't understand. He had told them of the dangers of Ouija boards and that he had learnt the hard way. They all kept their promise to him but it was a promise that I never had to make, and even if I did, I'm not sure whether my curiosity would have ever let me listen to his words of wisdom. Every one of us is entitled to an opinion and to discover things for themselves but what I have learnt from my own experiences is that there is no need to. If people can simply open up their minds, their beliefs and their trust in others, they would never have to see a planchette move with their own eyes, or the vision of a loved one asking for help to cross over. They would never have to endure the fear of knowing that because of some 'fun' they once had with a Ouija board, they now live in fear of what they contacted and whether it will stop at the physical manifestations and poltergeist activity. Because if it doesn't and you have to encounter the feeling of being touched, watched and possibly possessed by something that started out as a bit of harmless fun, you'll only wish you had taken the word of someone else.

If I can offer one piece of advice, that would be to listen to my late grandfather's words, a man who experienced every single level of paranormal activity; who endured years of frustration and lived in fear for his family. Make a promise to yourself that you too, will listen to some of what I have told you and take it as a lesson that some things are best left alone. Enjoy life whilst you have it and worry about death when it finds you.

However, if like me you did not start out by looking for answers and in fact the answers found you first, then pass your wisdom on to others, share your stories and experiences. Be laughed at sometimes, ridiculed even, but never take it to heart, it's just tough for some people to accept something which is not as clear as black or white, because that's one thing that the paranormal will never be. It will never be sanctimonious.

*****

Now I lay me down to sleep,
I pray the Lord my soul to keep,
If I shall die before I wake,
I pray the Lord my soul to take. Amen.
(Child's Christian Prayer)

Original painting, Richard Camp

16160350R00141

Printed in Great Britain
by Amazon